D1010694

* * *

PRAISE FOR
2017 CARNEGIE MEDAL NOMINEE
PAPER BUTTERFLIES

"A harrowing account of abuse, retaliation and love against all odds."

—*The Guardian*

"Heathfield has written a beautifully heartbreaking story that will frighten readers, tear them apart, give them hope, leave them hopeless, and, finally, give them some relief."

—*VOYA*

* * *

Flight of a Starling

Lisa Heathfield

carolrhoda LAB
MINNEAPOLIS

First American edition published in 2019 by Carolrhoda Lab™

First published in Great Britain in 2017 by Electric Monkey, an imprint of
Egmont UK Limited

Text copyright © 2017 by Lisa Heathfield

Carolrhoda Lab™ is a trademark of Lerner Publishing Group, Inc.

All US rights reserved. No part of this book may be reproduced, stored in
a retrieval system, or transmitted in any form or by any means—electronic,
mechanical, photocopying, recording, or otherwise—without the prior written
permission of Lerner Publishing Group, Inc., except for the inclusion of brief
quotations in an acknowledged review.

Carolrhoda Lab™
An imprint of Carolrhoda Books
A division of Lerner Publishing Group, Inc.
241 First Avenue North
Minneapolis, Minnesota 55401 USA

For reading levels and more information, look up this title at
www.lernerbooks.com.

Image credits: EditorAtLarge/Shutterstock.com (trapeze artist); Julia Poleeva/
Shutterstock.com (watercolor).

Main body text set in Janson Text LT Std 10.5/15.
Typeface provided by Linotype AG.

Library of Congress Cataloging-in-Publication Data

Names: Heathfield, Lisa, author.
Title: Flight of a starling / Lisa Heathfield.
Description: Minneapolis : Carolrhoda Lab, [2019] I Originally published:
    London : Electric Monkey, 2017. I Summary: Told from two viewpoints, sisters
    Lo and Rita spend their lives flying high on the trapeze, but real danger comes
    as secrets begin to unravel the tightknit circus community and Lo finds love
    with a "flattie."
Identifiers: LCCN 2018021916 (print) I LCCN 2018027930 (ebook) I
    ISBN 9781541541832 (eb pdf) I ISBN 9781541526112 (th : alk. paper)
Subjects: I CYAC: Sisters—Fiction. I Circus—Fiction. I Family life—Fiction. I
    Dating (Social customs)—Fiction.
Classification: LCC PZ7.1.H433 (ebook) I LCC PZ7.1.H433 Fli 2019 (print) I
    DDC [Fic]—dc23

LC record available at https://lccn.loc.gov/2018021916

Manufactured in the United States of America
1-44593-35505-6/22/2018

* * *

To Frank, Arthur, and Albert——
for being my extraordinary.

* * *

RITA

The air in the alley sticks to my skin. The bricks sit too close, pushing grief deeper into me. I stop to touch the walls.

Were you here, Lo?

I listen for a reply. Listen hard for her laughter, but it's not here. The silence grips so hard at my heart that I don't know how I breathe.

Dean stands waiting at the end of the alley, framed by daylight. It's only a few weeks since I've seen him, a few weeks since he was my sister's whispered secret, but he looks so different. Lo loved his eyes, but they're raw with a sadness I never knew could exist.

"Are you OK?" he asks, but he knows I'm not. Neither of us are.

"She really liked you," I say, my words stumbling in the bricked-in air. But he just stares at me, this boy from a world I don't know, a world that never moves on, unlike our circus.

"It's this way," is all he says. A building stands in front of us, and I know it's the abandoned factory that he came to with Lo. But she said it was beautiful, and it's not. It's gray and broken, and I feel cheated.

"Is this your mom's old factory?" I ask.

Dean looks surprised. "Lo told you?"

"She wanted me to see it."

I'm here now, Lo. But where are you?

The pain of missing her weighs on me, so heavy that I have to crouch down. I put my head into my hands, press so hard that my eyes hurt, dig my fingers deep into my skull until I can feel my hair pulling hard from my scalp.

I know Dean sits next to me. He moves my hands and puts them on the floor where Lo once walked. Then he stands up, this boy who burned so strong for her.

"This way," he says.

He leads me down the side of the factory, and we climb onto a rusting container and scramble through a hollow window. We're in the room that Lo described, with its low ceiling and empty squares where glass should be. I remember her eyes lighting up when she told me about it, and I thought I'd find a place sprinkled with rainbow ends.

I follow Dean up some stairs. Through a door and there's another with a lock that he opens. It's a small room and there's a painting on the wall in front of us, two people sitting on a cliff, a blur of birds above them.

"Did Lo come here?" I ask. *Did you leave your footprint?*

"She did this." He points to the wall next to us. There's a long blue line and standing on the end of it is a stick girl with a too-pink face and a big red mouth. "She's meant to be you."

"I'm smiling," I say.

A stick man has his arm around me. I know it's my dad.

Lo must have stood here, concentrating, but still she painted a leg too long. I imagine her laughing, looking away at the wrong time.

"Who's that?" I ask, pointing to a figure lying down on the line.

"Your grandpa. That's him too." The next figure is sitting up and has wide, round eyes. "And that one—that's your mom." The stick woman has been drawn in the same raggedy way, clumsy lines making her fall slightly from the wire. But her face is clear as daylight.

"You painted her face?"

"I just helped." Dean looks away.

"Why?"

"No reason." But there is. Lo has secrets hidden in this boy. On the end, there's a girl balancing tiptoe on the line.

"Lo," I say quietly, but Dean doesn't answer.

He's painted her with open arms, and she's smiling. Leaves are weaved into her hair, and birds are scattered around her hands. Feathered wings curve from her back and rise in an arc above her head.

"She's beautiful," I say.

Dean stands with his hands in his pockets. He has hurt and grief all folding in on themselves. Tears are on his cheeks, but I'm useless.

What should I do, Lo? How did you know him, when he's a stranger to me?

Without asking, I go to the row of cans underneath the painting. I look through the colors until I find the one that I want. The lid is difficult to get off, but I pull until it's free.

I want to paint it above Lo's head, but she's too tall, with her angel wings. So I hold the can next to her and spray it onto the wall, turning the drips into a clumsy red heart. In the middle I write "Lo". It's better than a footprint, I tell her. It won't disappear.

With the can in my hand I look at Dean.

"Where else did you go with her?" I ask him.

He hesitates for long enough for me to know that he doesn't want me walking in all their memories.

"The beach," he says.

"Let's go there." But before we leave, I lean my hand on Lo's wall. I want her angel wings to come alive and fold around me until I sleep and sleep and make it all go away. I need her to step out of the painting, her bare foot leaving the line and coming away from the bricks until she's standing here next to me.

But she doesn't, because she's not alive. And all I can do is kiss her painted cheek and silently beg to go back to before.

Chapter One

LO

Rita, Sarah, and I sprinkle sawdust over the waterlogged grass, making a path from our vans to the big top. Little chips that we scoop and throw, and I know when we're gone that they'll slowly get trodden down and disappear, just as we do.

Baby Stan, who's named after his dad, sits in the middle of us, his hands spread happy on the wet earth. Rita works in front of me, completely focused as she digs the spade into the wood shavings in the wheelbarrow, balancing it and throwing it steady onto the ground. She's always faster than me. I'm happy to hide behind the fact that she's eleven months older and must be stronger.

"You should slow down, Rites," I tell her.

"And you should put more clothes on." She laughs, pointing to the little gold top I'm wearing.

Sarah slaps a piece of shredded wood from Baby Stan's fingers.

"Not in your mouth," she says. For a moment, he looks

at his big sister from where he's sitting in the damp, deciding whether to cry, but she stares at him until he turns away. "Your hands are filthy," she tells him, even though she must know he isn't old enough to understand.

She reminds me so much of Ash when he was her age. The pale face with freckles that never disappear. Their mom, Carla, says she stewed their hair in a copper pot when they were born, but Ash shaves his head so close now that you can barely see the color.

The rain is light, but the drops are still batting into my eyes.

"Where's Spider when you need him?" I ask.

"You reckon friends can change the weather?" Rita asks.

"You never know. If he can eat fire, I reckon he can stop the rain."

"I bet Ash couldn't," Rita says.

"Don't you like him today?"

"No," Rita says firmly, but I just laugh at her. Ever since we were children, they've been in love, and we all know they're meant to be together, even if sometimes their relationship rocks unsteady. "I wish he'd marry a flattie."

Sarah looks shocked. "You don't mean that." She knows we're not allowed to be with people who don't have circus blood.

"You should be careful what you wish for," I tell Rita, as I scoop up the last scraps of sawdust from the wheelbarrow, throwing them high into the air, before we watch them settle, heavy and wet on the ground.

"Come on," Rita says. "Rob'll be waiting."

"Is he really going to put in the new motorbike trick?" Sarah asks.

"He says it'll bring in more people," Rita says.

"Will it be dangerous?"

"It has to be."

Sarah walks quickly to keep up, stopping with us as I balance the wheelbarrow against the props van.

"Tricks'll kill you if you leave that there," Rita tells me.

"I'll say it was you then." I laugh and link my arm through hers as we go into the big top.

"What's that?" Sarah asks. A huge bowl takes up almost the entire space of the performance ring. Its walls are made from a giant metal spider's web.

"Rob rented it," Rita says. Ash looks over and smiles when he hears her voice. He's standing next to Ernest, Spider's dad, and even though he's taller than him, he still looks like the boy we've grown up with. He's handsome too, and I wonder why Rita can even doubt him.

Dad's back is to us. "The risks are too high." He's an angel's breath shorter than Rob, but he's determined.

"It's what they want to see, or we lose them," Rob says.

"I think it looks exciting," Sarah says, and Dad turns to us.

"Lo and I are OK with it," Rita says, going to stand next to Rob.

"But I'm not sure I am," Dad says.

"It's no bigger a risk than anything else we do," Rob says, his hand on the seat of the motorbike. "It might look it, but the consequences are all the same."

"He's saying we could all die doing any one of our tricks." Ash laughs.

"You're not helping." Rob stares at him.

"It's not your daughters at risk, Rob," Dad says.

"But we've worked on it," Rob reassures him. "It won't go wrong."

"Won't it?"

"We're ready for it," I tell Dad. "We want to do it." I look at Rita and she nods.

"Why are you so worried this time?" Ma asks him.

"Because we haven't practiced enough," Dad answers. "This is the first time with the actual bowl, and he wants us to perform it in a couple of days."

"You've got to trust me," Rob insists. "It'll be worth it."

Ernest looks at Dad steadily. "It might be pushing it for us," he says, "but that doesn't mean it's not safe. It's just new." His wiry hair is pulled back in a ponytail, but stray bits still crackle out from his forehead. The teasing that he can't be Spider's dad, not looking so different, sometimes touches too much on true.

"We'll be OK, Dad," Rita says, linking her arm through his. "You're just getting nervous in your old age."

"Who are you calling old?" The smile he has can't cut out the worry, but it's enough for us to know he's backing down.

"Nerves are our enemy," Ernest reminds him.

But they're my friend too. They hold me before every jump. They're by my side and never really let me go, sending sparks through me and making my smile real.

"I think we should trust Rob," I say.

"Yes," Sarah says. She's desperate to impress, to be the center of the performance.

"Right then," Rob says quickly. "Let's try it out."

We follow him and Ernest as they push the motorbikes to the edge of the ring door curtains.

"So," Rob says, "Lo, remember you're not happy as the changeling, you want to get back to your world. That's the feeling you've got to get across to the audience."

I catch Rita's eye and pull a face.

"It's not funny, Lo," Rob says seriously. "Just going through the motions isn't enough. You've got to actually feel it, make the audience really believe."

"Yes, boss."

"I'm not the boss."

"He certainly isn't," Ernest says. "He's just a young pretender."

But there's warmth in his voice. Most flatties who join us only stay for a few months, but Rob has been with us four years, and he's woven into our circus fabric now.

"You ready, fairy queen?" I ask Rita.

"Of course," she smiles, before she puts on her helmet, clicking it firmly into place.

Rob and Ma sit on one motorbike. They pull down their black visors together, blocking themselves off from us. Dad stands to the side with Sarah and Ash, watching as Rita and I climb onto the other bike behind Ernest. I have to crouch at the back and steady myself, before I pull my own helmet over my head.

Immediately, the sounds are numbed. Inside it, the world shrinks to just me.

Ernest turns to us. "Ready?"

"Yes." I think the word stays trapped in the mask and so I nod.

"Ten laps, then Rita, you jump onto Rob's motorbike. Two more, then it's you, Lo. They're quick, so count. Don't forget," he says. "OK?" And I nod before he pulls down his visor.

We've been over and over it, and it's locked in my mind. Still, I run through it, the exact pressure from my feet, where my hands must be.

Rob and Ernest start the engines, filling the big top with the noise of the bikes. I hold Rita tight as we race and tip toward the edge of the wall down into the bowl. From here, it's beautiful, a perfect crater, a metal web for the future audience to see through.

We drop into it, and the speed is instant. One lap. Ma and Rob rush past us, head on, the fronts of our bikes almost scraping. Two laps. If I reached out, I could touch them. Three. I count as the wheels leap up above the edge, a mirror to them, air beneath us. My blood has become fire. I count the rest of the laps, each one burning adrenaline deeper into me.

Rob comes close, and Rita leaps onto their bike. I'm not meant to look, but I do. For long seconds the noise cradles her, before she's caught by Ma and she's safe.

One more lap.

"Go!" I hear Ernest shout.

I don't have time to think, only jump in the way Rob's taught me, enough to reach them.

In one breath, everything is washed silent, before the world is back, and I land behind Rita.

But I've misjudged it. I know as soon as my foot hits the seat that it's in the wrong place; the bike will unbalance. It tips too far to the side and Rita falls. Ma swings out an arm for her, but Rita crashes onto the metal and spins away from us.

I try to jump for her, but Ma grabs me. She holds me until the bike stops on the ledge, and I see Rita, curled too far away. We run, and when I get to her there's blood on my sister, twisting in ribbons up her arm. I try to say her name, but my breathing swallows it.

Ash stands motionless as Ma kneels next to her, and Dad is taking the helmet gently from her head. Rita's eyes are open. Her curls are smeared against her skin and shock is covering her face, but she's breathing. The world starts ticking again as I take off my helmet.

"Rita?" I crouch down, scared to touch her.

"It went a bit wrong," she smiles weakly, her words lopsided.

"Does anything hurt apart from your arm?" Dad asks her. She shakes her head. "And can you move your legs?"

"Yes," she replies. So he puts his arms under her, carefully lifts her, and carries her quickly up the edge of the crater. Now I hold my sister's hand. The skin from her shoulder to her elbow is grazed and packed with blood.

"Your arm's a mess," I tell her.

"At least it's not my face."

"Not the face," I say. And her laughter is enough.

★ ★ ★

We don't light the barrel fire. It feels wrong to do it until Rita is back safe with us. Instead, we sit in Ernest and Helen's van, waiting for more news.

"Why haven't they phoned again?" Rob is pacing up and down through the center of us all.

"It doesn't mean anything is wrong," Ernest says. "Just that they're busy." I know he's saying the words for me too, using ones that I need to hear. Spider and I were born within days of each other, so his parents treat me almost like their own.

"And she's not concussed," Helen says. "Ray said they just need to check that nothing's broken."

I imagine the camera looking through to my sister's bones, and in my mind I make them a smooth white with no chips or cracks.

"She'll be OK, Lo," Spider tells me, squeezing my hand.

"It's not your fault, Rob," Ernest tells him. "Things go wrong."

11

"Rita could've died," Rob says.

"But she didn't," I remind him. He shouldn't feel guilty about this. He only pushes us because he wants our circus to survive.

"You made her wear the helmet. You made us all do that, so in a way you saved her."

"I'm not sure your dad will see it like that," Ash says. He's ripping little shreds of white paper and chewing them into balls. He spits them careless into his hand and drops them in the waste bin. I'm glad Stan and Carla have taken Sarah back to their van, so she won't see him looking so worried.

"Spider says she's going to be OK, Ash," I tell him, but I'm speaking quickly, trying to wash away my own guilt. If I had landed properly, if I had got it right, then Rita would be safe with us now.

Ash looks up at Rob, lets his eyes follow his pacing. "The flatties don't need so much danger when they come to see us."

"I think they do," Rob says.

"So you're still going to keep in the motorbikes?" Ash asks. Rob looks so briefly at me that I doubt he sees me nod.

"Yes," he says.

Spider's mom takes a thick cloth from a hook and reaches into the oven. She pulls out two trays covered in steam, and a sweet smell clings to the room. No one says a word as she picks out her thin china plates from the cupboard. Her spoon sinks deep and steady through the bread pudding.

"Spider," she says, without looking up. "Pass it 'round." And he gets up.

I've never once seen him falter in his mom's demands. Ernest and Helen wanted children enough to line the tent with but were blessed only with Spider. Sometimes I think their dreams for him are too heavy on his shoulders. Sometimes I imagine lifting them off bit by bit and letting the real Spider roam free.

He passes me a plate. I don't want to have it, not without Rita here, and I know I won't feel like it until she walks through the door. But I've been given the food, and so I must eat, the sugar tasteless on my tongue.

It's ten o'clock when Ash and I see the lights of Dad's car swing into their place. We turn from looking through the window and run out of the door, jumping down the steps in one and getting to the car as it's still ticking hot.

Rita's face looks tired through the window, but she's smiling.

I open the door, but it's Ash she's looking at, and it makes everything feel uneven.

"Are you OK?" he asks her, reaching in to hold her hand.

"I'm fine," she says. She has Dad's jacket perched big on her shoulders, a white fabric bandage winding thick up her arm.

"Let's get you into Terini," Ma says, leading us across the grass toward mine and Rita's van, stopped next to theirs.

"You could've at least broken it," I say to Rita, prodding her better arm.

"I wish I had," she says. "Instead I'm going to have a scar like a wrinkled old prune."

"It'll match your face nice, then," Ash smiles, and he kisses her quick on the lips before she can protest. It's the first time he's kissed her like that where Ma and Dad can see, and it makes the dark air prickle awkward.

"They'll be turning in early tonight," Dad tells Ash, as we get to the steps of Terini.

"Oh, OK." Ash doesn't take his eyes from our Rita. "You sure you're all right?" he asks her.

"I'm fine."

"Good," he says earnestly. "I hope it doesn't hurt too much."

"I can't feel a thing," she laughs. "Not with all the painkillers."

"If you're sure then," Ash says. "I'll say goodnight."

"Goodnight," Rita says, and Ma is already pushing her fast through the door.

"Night, Ash." I hug him tight and feel the last of his worry dissolve, before I climb the van's steps and shut our door to the world.

Inside, Ma is pulling back the duvet on Rita's top bunk. "Lo, promise me you'll come and get me from our van if Rita needs me," she says.

"I will. I promise."

"I'm not happy about leaving you for the night," Ma says.

"I'm fine, Ma," Rita tells her. "I'm just going to sleep."

"You're only next door, Ma," I remind her.

"Don't keep her chatting all night, Lo. She needs to rest." Even at her most stern, Ma's face is still beautiful.

"I'll be quiet as a mouse," I laugh.

"OK," she says, tucking Rita's curl gently behind her ear. "You sure?"

"Night, Ma," Rita says, hugging her and pushing her out of the door, closing it so that it's only us.

"Ash was worried," I tell Rita, as she pulls her bandaged arm through the sleeve of her top.

"Was he?"

"Of course he was. He's good through and through, your Ash," I say.

"*My* Ash?"

"You know he is, Rita."

And she replies with only a smile.

RITA

We moved on yesterday, so my arm has had a day to recover, but Ma still brought my breakfast to Terini this morning. I don't go to Mada until lunchtime, and now they flit around me, making me sit at the table and not letting me help at all.

"My arm's not that bad," I say. "I'd like to do something at least." It doesn't feel right to sit here watching Ma and Lo do all the work.

"Make the most of it." Ma smiles at me as she puts a plate of chicken cutlets in front of me.

"It makes a nice change to see you sitting down," Gramps says. He's in his armchair as he likes, his tray of food balanced on his lap. It's only been a year since Lo and I moved into our own van, to make space for Gramps in here, but now I can't imagine him anywhere else.

"It's a strange town, this one," I say.

"Why?" Ma asks, as she pours gravy from the pan into the jug.

"It's just got a funny feel to it," I say. Lo puts her plate next to Dad, and he moves to make room.

"We've only been here a day," Ma says. "You've hardly seen it." She wipes at the edge of her mouth with the napkin. A bit of her lipstick sticks to the material.

"It's just strange," I say. "And there's not much of a view, either." Sometimes we're next to fields and hills, but now the window by the sink looks out on the wall at the edge of the park.

"Not like the pitch near Haworth," Dad says. "Do you remember those sunsets across the moors, Liz?"

Ma screws up her face. "With those wild horses that stuck their noses through our windows?" She's already done her hair, even though it's early, some dark curls trapped in a knot, the rest falling by her neck.

"We should've kept one," I say.

"They're meant to be free," Lo says. She balances a pea on the side of her plate and flicks it at me. But I'm too quick and catch it in my fingers.

"Too slow, Bozo," I laugh. She picks up two more, but Dad clamps his hand over hers.

"Don't waste food, Lo."

"It's only two peas, Dad." But she's laughing as she throws them into her mouth, smiling widely so that I can see them held squashed between her teeth.

"Nice," I say.

"Like your mangled arm," she says.

"Lo." Ma's not smiling any more.

"It's not mangled," I say. "Look, it moves and everything." I bend it crooked at the elbow, then stretch it out to wiggle my fingers.

"I think that Rob is pushing you too far," Gramps says, laying his knife and fork neatly on his plate.

"He knows what he's doing," I say.

"Does he?" Gramps asks. Although it was before Rob's time, memories of Gran Margaret whisper around us, her accident never far from Gramps's eyes.

"Nothing bad will happen to us," I tell him. "Rob cares about us too much to put us in real danger." Lo told me how he paced up and down last night, his thoughts filled with me.

"Are you definitely all right to perform?" Lo asks, serious

now. Blame isn't a word we use in our circus, but deep inside her, I can tell that guilt still flickers.

"Course," I say. "Besides, it's only set-up today."

"You're not to do any heavy lifting," Dad tells me.

"I'd better look after her then," Lo tries, but Dad just clips her gently around the head.

"You, Miss Lolita, will have to work twice as hard."

LO

With set-up finally finished, Rita and I go to find the barrel fire. Rob is already there in the darkness sitting on his stool, Spider on the carved log next to him. Sarah sits cross-legged on the grass, watching as Ash throws some wood in and pokes at the flames with a stick.

"I'm just saying, he shouldn't have done it," Rob says.

"Who's done what?" I ask, unhooking Rita's arm from mine. Rob moves up for us, and we sit next to him on the stretch of log by the warmth.

"You don't need to know," Spider says.

"I don't need to, but I want to," I say, yet his silence is the only answer I get.

The dark edges of the park sit behind us, watching the back of my jacket sewn with a dragon's head, its fire-breath winding up my sleeve.

Tips of orange burn out of the barrel as Ash sits down.

"When you going to be my bride, Rita?" he asks as he does every time.

"Never," she replies.

I laugh. "You will, Rites."

Rob chuckles and spits at his feet.

"Are you coming to see the town with us?" Spider asks him.

"I'll leave you younger ones to enjoy it alone tonight," Rob says.

"You're not much older," Rita tells him, tipping her head slightly as she looks at him. When Rob joined us, I couldn't tell his age. He slipped between us and our parents, and I know he's really somewhere in between.

"Ready to go?" Ash asks, his eyes only for Rita.

"Maybe," she says, although she knows she will. We have to explore. If we didn't, I tell her, our souls will shrivel up and die.

"Should you go out with your arm still bad?" Rob asks her.

"It's loads better already," she says, giving him a smile to wash away his guilt.

"Can I come?" Sarah asks, wide-eyed in the flame light.

"You shouldn't even still be awake." Ash ruffles his sister's hair, and she ducks away from him, making it neat again.

"It won't be long before you join us," I tell her.

"And you're not exactly missing much," Rita adds.

"Don't be back late," Rob says, leaning forward with his elbows on his knees. The fire-shine catches on one cheek, the other in shadow. "It'll be an early start." He picks up a leaf and starts slowly shredding it, dropping each section to the ground when he's done.

"We won't be," Rita says.

I stretch my legs out in front of me, my arms straight to the solid black sky. The warmth from the fire touches the line of my bare belly, between my top and my jeans.

"It's endless up there," I say, as my bracelets clink down on each other. They sound like stars falling.

"We should get going then," Ash says. He stands up and puts his hands out toward Rita. She lets him pull her to her feet but won't keep her fire-warmed palm in his.

"Sure you don't want to come?" Spider asks Rob.

"I'm staying here," he says, still staring into the flames.

"Suit yourself," I say, grabbing Spider's hand to pull myself up. "See you later."

We walk across the darkening grass, Rita linking her arm through mine. Two boys cut close nearby on bikes, hats low on their heads. They stare at us for too long, and I wonder if our circus blood somehow sits on the outside of our skin. Spider starts to walk more quickly, so we stay with him and Ash until we're by the road and we follow the direction the few cars are headed as they thread through the night.

"This place gives me the creeps," Rita says.

"It's OK," I say.

"Nah. There's something rotten in the air."

"You won't think that when people pay to come and see you prancing around in your feathers," Ash says.

"Fair enough."

We cross the road at the traffic lights, and the stores on either side are ones we've seen a thousand times before. It's too late for them to be open, but there're still people around.

"I bet they're all ghosts," I say.

"I don't care, as long as they've lots of cash to make us rich," Spider says.

"We'll never be rich, Spides," I say. Even with Rob's new ideas, every year fewer people come to see us.

"It's definitely got grimy air," Rita says.

"We won't be stopping long," I remind her.

"Lil said no good was coming. Maybe it's here that it's going to happen," Rita says.

"Lil spouts baloney," Ash reminds her, and I know he's right. Lil, with her ancient van and cards she can't really read.

"No more than you," she says. Ash looks hurt. He must feel like a boat cut loose—one day Rita is kissing him, the next she doesn't want to know.

The line of stores moves outward, curving around a large

fountain stuck in the concrete. It reaches high, its water tumbling in prickling lines.

"There's something nice," I say, pointing toward it.

"The water or the forbidden flattie boys?" Rita asks. Sitting on the edge are three of them. They watch us as we get closer. They were talking, but now they're quiet.

"Evening," I say.

"Evening," the boy nearest us says, a hat tight down over his eyes while the other two just nod.

"Lost your tongues?" I ask, but my words have no sharp edges to them.

"Hi," the boy next to him says, his face cracked through with acne scars. I bet Lil's cream could sort him out. The boy at the end with the stud through his ear stays silent.

I lean over the stone ledge and put the tips of my fingers into the bubbling water. Beneath the foam is a scatter of coins. If these boys weren't here, I know what I would be doing now.

Spider and Ash look like they want to keep walking, but I sit down and catch my hand in the falling tracks of spray.

The nearest boy takes off his hat, and there's an instant pull inside me. Dad always told me it's best not to look at a flattie too long, but I've never seen one like this. He's got cheekbones you could balance cups on. And Ma says curls on a boy mean he's honest, so I figure his blood is true through and through.

"You're not from around here?" he asks. He has hair the same deep brown as Spider's.

"No," I say. "We're with the circus."

"Serious?" the middle boy asks. "The one in East Park?"

"I don't know if it's east, but it's a park," I say.

"You must've seen the posters," the same boy says to the other two. "The one with the angel on it."

"It's a changeling," Rita tells him.

"A what?"

"A fairy left in place of a stolen child," the nearest boy says.

"How d'you know that?" the boy on the end laughs.

"But in our circus, it's the changeling who wants to get back to her home," Rita says.

"It looks like an angel on the poster," he says.

"They're the same thing," I tell him. "Didn't you know?"

"It's not like a normal circus then?" the nearest boy says. He's looking right at me as he speaks.

"It's more frightening," I say, willing him to look away first, but he doesn't.

"Do you do all the normal stuff, though?" the middle boy asks.

"You'll have to come and see," I reply.

"We should get going," Ash says, stepping closer to Rita.

"We've only just got here, Ash. You can go if you want," I tell him. "Rita and I won't be long."

"You can't stay on your own," Spider says. "Your mom would kill us."

"We're not on our own," I say. But Ash and Spider don't move.

"Is there a clown then?" the middle boy asks. I touch my finger to my eye as quick as I can, and I know the others do it too. "What are you doing?" he asks, uneasy.

"Superstition." I regret it as soon as I say it. I don't want them walking into our world.

"I'm Dean," the boy nearest us says. He puts out his hand to shake mine, all formal. I have to take my fingers from the water and wipe the damp across my jeans.

Dean. I take his name and wrap it and unwrap it in my head.

"Lo," I say.

"Is that your real name?" he asks.

"No. Laura is." He doesn't speak, but he nods his head and has a smile that says he likes it. "This is Rita," I say, and he shakes her hand too, staring right into her eyes in a way that makes my stomach flip with jealousy.

"I'm Will," the boy next to him says, leaning across to shake Rita's hand and then mine.

"Paul," the boy with the earring says, tipping his finger to his forehead in a mini salute.

"What's it like then, this town?" I ask, as Spider shuffles his feet and Ash steps even closer to Rita's side.

"It's all right," Will says. "What's it like in the circus?"

"It's all right." I mimic his words.

"It's everything," Rita says.

Dean sort of squints at the pair of us.

"Are you two sisters?" he asks.

"Rita's older," I say.

"Only by eleven months," she reminds me.

"And the sensibilist."

"Is that even a word, Lo?" Rita laughs.

Dean wears a denim jacket that looks battered by too many years. Underneath it, his white T-shirt is clean. His finger-nails are cut properly and clean too. Ma would approve, if he wasn't a flattie.

"Are you brothers?" I smile at all of them.

"Nah," Will says. "I'm too good-looking to be related to them." A group of girls walk past, their heels clicking on the concrete.

I like their laughter. It almost swallows them whole.

"What's it really like?" The look Dean gives me swoops

down into my bones. "Traveling all the time?"

"It's what we know," I say. I won't tell these strangers how sometimes I wonder if I want more. That maybe the circus isn't always enough.

"It's home," Ash says.

"But you're always moving."

"The outside isn't home. It's the inside," Rita says. "Inside the vans and inside us."

"We like it," Ash says from next to her. He hovers like a crow.

"I think you're lucky," Paul says. He's perched on the end, leaning far enough forward so the conversation reaches him.

"So do we," Rita says.

"What's it like staying in one place all the time?" I ask.

"Boring," chips in Will. "I wouldn't mind coming with you." The way his eyes are on me makes me feel naked.

"We don't let just anybody in," Ash says.

"Were you born into it then?" Dean asks. I feel safer with him looking at me.

"Yes," I say. "And our mom and dad before us."

"They're circus born and bred?" Will asks.

"And proud of it," Ash tells him.

"Why wouldn't they be?" Dean looks up at him. "It sounds like a good way of life." Ash only pushes his hands back into his pockets and shrugs.

I put my hand palm down into the water. I turn to kneel on the edge and then tip myself over. I splash into the cold wet, my feet the last to disappear.

Under here, I can't see or hear anyone. In the blackness, I feel the grainy floor of the fountain, my fingers brushing past circles of coins. When I can no longer breathe, I go back, my head breaking through the bubbles on the surface.

"I've got one," I say, holding my hand high in the air.

"What are you doing?" Paul sounds uncertain as he looks around. I wipe the water from my eyes.

"I had to get a lucky coin," I say. I pull my slippery self back onto the ledge and squeeze more water from me, the dragon's fiery tongue dripping icy wet from my sleeve.

The coin in my palm is a one pence piece.

"It'll protect you from this spooky town," Rita says, as I close my fingers around it, feeling my jeans cling cold to me now.

"You think it's a spooky town?" Dean asks her, but he's looking at me.

"I like it here," I say.

"You must be freezing, Lo," Rita says, ignoring him. She links her arm through mine and immediately I feel the fountain's water sinking through my top.

"Best get home," Spider says, and as Rita gets up, she pulls me with her.

"It was nice to meet you," Dean says. He's smiling at me.

"And you," Rita says.

"Will we see you again?" he asks. The boys I know aren't like him, and I want to pull him with us and keep him close to me as the sky turns light.

"Come to the show," I say before we walk away, the fountain's water dripping from me, my lucky coin curled into my palm.

RITA

"Your hair is still wet," I tell Lo. "Ma would kill you if she saw you going to bed like that."

"Then it's a bit of luck we've got our own van," she says, squeezing her bangs tight in her hand. "Look, no drips. I'll be fine."

She puts her clothes in our tiny bathroom, hanging crooked over the toilet seat.

"Are you cold?" I ask.

"You're fussing," Lo says, jumping into her bed and running her legs quick under her duvet. "I'm toasty as toast."

"What imaginative words you have," I laugh, pulling myself over the bottom rungs of our ladder to get into the bunk above her.

"All the better to eat you with."

"Words don't eat, Lo."

"The knife and fork ones do." Her laughter fills our bedroom. There's something different about her since we went out and met those boys, something fizzing under her skin.

"Which one was it then?" I ask.

"Which what?"

"Don't pretend you don't know. Which boy did you like?"

"Which boy where?"

"Lo."

She pauses. I hear her scratch the slats of my bed as she always does before she tells me a secret.

"Dean," she says.

"The one with the hat?"

"Mm."

"Just mm?"

"Mm mm."

"I see."

In the silence, I can hear the water from Lo's clothes dripping onto the toilet seat. They'll be hanging there, dark from the wet, and I know they'll never be dry by morning.

"What did it feel like?" I ask. "When you first saw him?" I want to know if burning hearts are true.

"It felt like the air stopped."

I don't want to be jealous, but I am.

"But he's a flattie."

"I know."

I click off the lamp that Dad fixed to the edge of my bed, the lead hanging down all the way past Lo.

"I want to see him again, Rita."

"You know Dad won't approve."

"I won't tell him."

I hear her turn over in her bed. She's stopped kicking her legs, so I hope the cold has left her.

"Does it feel different? To you and Spider?"

"Yes, completely," she says. "More like you and Ash."

"I've told you, I don't like him right now."

"But why not? Anyone can see you're meant to be together. You're lucky."

"Am I?"

"Of course you are," she says, yet the happy parts have gone from her voice. "At least you can be with Ash if you want to be."

"Don't be sad, Lo."

"I'm not." But I hear her breath weighed heavy in the dark.

Chapter Two

LO

"Your breakfast is getting cold. Hurry up, the pair of you." Ma throws my jeans onto the bed. "Or Dad will start eating it," she says over her shoulder as she goes out of our bedroom and closes the front door behind her.

"We should take her key away," I say.

"What, ban her from Terini?" Rita asks.

"It's our space. What's the point of moving out of Mada if they can just come in when they want?" I poke my hands into the wooden slats of her bed above me.

"You try telling Ma that," Rita says. Her mattress huffs, and I imagine her pulling the duvet tight around her.

"Maybe not."

I bring my legs around the bottom of the ladder, touching it three times with my thumb to keep the witch in there sleeping. She walked straight out of a storybook Ma read us one day, and now she sits too often waiting to scratch our ankles.

"Those boys last night," I say, standing on tiptoes and reaching to the ceiling.

"Are you still thinking about him?"

"Girls!" Dad shouts from the steps of their van.

"Keep your hair on," Rita muffles into her pillow. But there'll be bacon frying, and that's enough to make me dress quick and take me out of Terini and into Mada's kitchen.

"Morning, Gramps," I say. He's always the first person we go to, sitting deep in his armchair. He puts down his book to give me a kiss.

"Morning, love."

"What was the town like?" Ma asks. She's washing up hurriedly in the sink.

"Quiet," I say.

"Just quiet?"

"Everything was shut. We just walked around."

"Just you and Rita?" She stops to look over her shoulder at me.

"And Spides and Ash. We met a couple of locals. And I went swimming in the fountain."

Ma doesn't react. I wonder if she's even heard, as she scrubs the sponge so hard around the mug that I'm surprised she doesn't wear the china away.

★ ★ ★

The rain pounds on the roof of our empty big top, its noise echoing heavy inside, filling up even the tiniest spaces.

"It better have stopped by later," Rita says. "Or the music will get swallowed."

"By a rain beast?" I ask, raising my eyebrow at her.

"Exactly," she says.

Between us, her costume sits on the ground, the snagged material needing to be tucked under and sewn. I'm unpicking a feather stuck in the way of the thread and don't notice Rob before he's standing next to us.

"That doesn't exactly need two of you," he says.

"It's because of her arm," I tell him, smiling up at him. "She can't possibly do this on her own." He knows it's not true. Lil insisted on curing Rita with one of her creams and the skin is healing quick.

"Join us if you like?" Rita asks, though he wouldn't be much help.

"No time," he says. "Tricks is making me double-check the bike engine."

"I could help you when we've finished this," Rita says, but she's talking to the back of his coat, as he's already walking away from us and through the ring door curtains.

I hold the needle careful in my fingers, wet the end of the thread with my mouth before looping it through. The rain still beats down above us.

"Do you really think we're lucky?" I ask Rita. "That we live like this."

"Of course," she says. "Why would you ask that?"

"I don't know. I've just been thinking, that's all."

"Then don't," she says, sounding just like Ma. "Because we don't fit anywhere else."

I twist the thread into a knot and don't say any more.

My make-up is so heavy I can barely open my eyes, gold glitter dancing across my cheekbones. I've threaded the feathers into my hair and stepped into the sequined suit of my changeling skin.

For this part, I put the thin white dress over the top, its sleeves dipped in beads, and I loop my arms into the elastic of my purple wings so that they stretch out across my back.

I never look in the mirror when I'm in my costume—I once told Rita that the reflection of the fallen angel would step out and stick to her forever, and I made myself believe it too.

I run across the muddy ground and up the wooden steps of Lil's van. Inside, it's almost dark. She's sitting behind her table in her little wicker chair, the end of her cigarette glowing a pinprick of color.

"Lucky I wasn't Tricks," I say. "Finding you smoking when customers are about to come in."

"What customers?" The smoke twists and bends into the deep lines of her skin.

"He'd sooner set you alight than see you smoking in front of them," I say.

She flicks ash into the bowl of water before her, her laugh collapsing into a cough that gets stuck in her closed mouth. When she opens her lips, it's to spit phlegm into her handkerchief, which she tucks into her sleeve.

"You wouldn't tell though, would you, little Laura?"

"What's it worth?" I laugh, and she swats at me with a hand spotted with rings. I click the lamp on by her feet, and a small light shivers up toward her face, leaving her eyes as hollow holes.

"Get the customers in, girl. Let's get the cash rolling and grow rich enough to live like queens."

Outside, the sky is thick with clouds, but my eyes sting slightly in the daylight. We're next to the entrance of the big top, and I beckon to strangers with my long fingernails dipped in color. There are droplets of fear in their eyes, before they look away, and I want to tell them that I'm nothing like this really, that if they looked carefully, they'd see just me.

I'm spreading my wings high above me in an arc, watching the feathers mingling with the beads, when I hear people speaking.

"It is one of them," a voice says. I turn, and it's two of the boys from the fountain. Dean and Will. They come right up close.

"You look different," Dean says to me, making my heart quick.

"You don't," I say, and I smile back at him, even though our angels are meant to keep a face blank of everything.

"What's this then?" Will points his thumb to the closed van behind us.

"It's your destiny," I say, and they both laugh.

"A fortune teller?" Will asks.

"More than that." I look steady into Dean's eyes.

"What do we have to do then?" he asks.

"You're not going in?" Will pokes his arm.

"Why not?" Dean says. "It's always good to know what the future has in store."

"It'll be a load of nonsense."

Dean ignores him. "How much is it?"

"Three of your finest gold coins."

"Three pounds!" Will says.

"I'll meet you here," Dean tells him.

Within my angel costume, I can watch as he puts his hands into his jeans and pulls out some money.

"Suit yourself," Will says. "I'll just be here alone while you waste your money."

I lead Dean up the steps, open the door, and we go inside. Lil sits motionless.

"Is there anyone there?" she asks. Dean looks at me, a half smile on his lips. I have to look away.

"She's blind," I tell him, but for the first time ever I don't like the lie. "She feels the future with her soul." I've said the words a hundred times before.

"Right," Dean says.

"A boy," Lil says, her voice lower than before, a whisper in her lamplight.

She holds out her hands, palms up. Dean only looks at me.

"I can't touch your money," I tell him. "You need to give it to her." He steps forward hesitantly, and I hear the sound of his coins settling onto her skin and dropping into a pocket lost in her skirt.

He's awkward as she holds his hand. In her other, she takes mine. I look away from Dean again. He's made everything feel different, and now we're linked, almost touching.

"Your angel will choose a number," Lil says.

"Six," I reply.

Lil stares deep at him with her cave-like eyes and counts out the cards onto the table. As always, it's the picture of an angel's wing. Dean studies it so earnestly that I want to tell him that none of this is true.

"There are obstacles in your path, but you have hidden wings that will help you," she says, as Dean nods solemnly. "But worry is weighing you down." Lil looks at nothing. "Am I right?"

"Um. Kind of," Dean says.

"I feel there is light, though," Lil says, her voice hazy. "Yes, there is light."

Dean looks at me. "Three pounds," he mouths, but he doesn't seem angry.

I take his hand before Lil can stop me. She's meant to be blind, so she can't pretend she can suddenly see. There is a painted door at the back of her van, and I lead him through. Inside, it's no bigger than a cupboard, and it's completely dark. Any outside sounds are muffled into almost silence.

"What are we doing here?" Dean asks. He has the remnants of a laugh in his voice, but it's unsteady.

"Are you scared?" I ask, the angel dropping from me.

"No." His voice is so close to me, sitting just on my skin as he speaks.

"I want to know what frightens you."

The air has never felt like this. If I move, I think it might burn me.

"What frightens me?"

"Yes," I whisper.

"Is this in the old woman's script?"

I wonder if he hears my heart beating.

"Name three things."

"OK," he says. "Cotton wool."

"Cotton wool?"

"I don't like the way it sounds when I touch it." I can tell he's smiling, his words tipping up.

"Lo?" It's Lil's voice, drifting urgent through the door.

"A bigger fear than that," I tell him.

There's a pause, where the darkness swells tight between us.

"I'm frightened that something will happen to my mom."

I struggle to find an answer.

"Nothing will happen to her," I say, as if I know, as if I really can read Lil's cards.

"How are you so sure?" he asks.

"I just am. She won't die before her time."

I move slightly, and I think the feathers of my wings brush against him.

"Lo." Lil sounds angry now. "His time is up."

"The third thing you're scared of?" I ask quickly. I can feel him pause.

"You," he says.

"Me?"

"Yes."

The door opens and dim light scuttles in, bringing Lil with it.

"Enough," she says, her eyes clearly seeing into the room. Dean looks awkward, unsure what to do. I know he watches me as I walk past him, and he follows me to the van's front door. Outside, Will is leaning against the steps.

"Did you get your money's worth?" he asks, smiling wide at Dean.

"Of course," I say, before Dean can reply, and I leave them and go back in.

Lil is sitting in her chair in the silence, laying her cards of angel wings face down on the table. When she looks up, her eyes cloud with the future.

"Be careful, Lo," she says.

★ ★ ★

The audience doesn't know that Rita and I are here, crouched like lions way above their heads. The curtained ledge we're hiding on barely fits us both, tucked high into the roof of our big top.

"I think you should just marry Ash," I whisper, even though the music filling the tent will easily cover my words. "Say you will, or I'll dive from here." I pull back the curtain until a small slice of light streaks steady across Rita's face. "Say you will." I shuffle closer to the edge, her red fairy wings brushing like water against my arm.

"Don't be daft, Lo." There's no fear in her eyes. She knows I'll never jump.

"Ma was eighteen when she married Dad. You've only a few months left to match that."

"I don't want to match it."

"You do," I insist. She looks older here, dressed as the fairy queen, her make-up thick and deep on her skin, purple feathers weaved tight into her hair. "Don't you love him?"

"Of course I love him. But maybe like a brother." She looks at me so seriously, leading our words to a different place. "And I don't know if that's enough."

"What do you mean?" I ask, as the music runs circles around the bright lights just beyond us.

"Maybe he's too young."

"He's the same age as you."

"Sometimes I think I'd like someone a bit older."

"Who?" I ask.

But the crack of false thunder spears the inside of the big top and spins everything into darkness. Instantly there's the feeling I have at the beginning of every performance, as adrenaline makes my blood beat. My heart ticks quietly under the sequins clinging close to my skin.

"Good luck, sister," Rita whispers. I reply by kissing my finger and touching her nose, managing it the first time. With me, she misses, and her nail skims close to my eye. I'm laughing when I shouldn't be, and I hear her trying to hush me.

Through the gap in the curtain flashes of lightning show an empty hoop high above the audience's heads. I wonder if Dean is among them, looking up, waiting.

"Go," Rita says, and I move to the edge, careful not to knock against her healing arm. I push back the heavy material and, as the fairy child, I jump.

In the air, I reach out and grab onto the hanging hoop. It jolts my arms, but I don't let them know. Darkness again, and I swing up my body, curl balanced in the floating circle. With each crash of white, I change position. One second they see me with my wings spread wide, the next my body bent almost in two.

A drumbeat of music shows Rita jumping high through the air, a wash of dark feathers. I cower, trapped, as she twists up next to me.

"Fancy meeting you here," I whisper, my lips unmoving. She widens her eyes to tell me to be quiet, before she lets her body fall back, contorting herself over the circle like melted wax. And then my gentle older sister pulls herself up and pushes me from the hoop.

Even with the music, I hear the audience's gasp, sharp around us. They didn't see me hook the rope so that I spin safely down, the fairy child forced to earth.

I let go and step lightly onto the floor, where Sarah sits in front of me. She looks much younger than her eleven years, her golden-red hair tied back, her clothes matching the rag doll on her lap. She doesn't look up as the music builds, doesn't notice the angels creeping around her, Ernest and Helen with their faces covered in silver gauze, arms stuck tight with feathers.

They're fairies waiting to steal the human child, juggling rings of fire in the air as they move. Sarah doesn't see the net they throw over her until it's too late.

Her screams fill the big top, as Dad lowers Rita's hoop quick to the floor, and the fairy queen steals the human child, taking her spinning to the roof. The rag doll falls by my feet. Faceless angels step toward me, ready to cut me from myself.

Does Dean watch as they rip my wings, strip feathers violent from my arms? Is he here? Slowly, I disappear, forced to become a changeling.

* * *

With no music, no audience left, we can hear the rain fall heavy on the roof of the costume tent.

"Would you listen to that?" Stan says, wiping cotton wool rough across his cheeks. When he stretches the greasepaint from his eyes he looks as old as my dad again, the age-lines not hidden any more.

"Shame for the people walking home through it." Helen unhooks the sleeves from her costume, the sequined skin shredded into her palm.

"I like the sound of it, though," I say, as Ma squeezes in beside me, making too many of us in the small space.

"Don't go thinking you can go out in it," she laughs.

"I won't be long," I say, turning from her and running back down the tunnel.

"Lo," she says, but she doesn't try to stop me. Through the gap to the outside, the sky is clogged heavy with clouds. The rain batters the ground, and even though I'm still dressed as a changeling, I run into it. Already the grass has caught puddles.

"Rita!" I call out, although I know she's not close by. But I wish she were here with me, holding hands as children again, when there was nothing more important than the rain hitting our arms and our eyelashes and spreading under our feet.

I glance around, wanting to see Dean, this boy I barely know, a stranger whose life stays still. I want him to look at me in that way again. Even though I shouldn't, as we've always been told that flatties only bring trouble.

"Lo! Get inside!" The voice is muffled through the stamping water, but I know it's Tricks.

I spin one more time, close my eyes to the dripped-down sky, before I run into the dry. "What the hell are you doing? There could be punters still around." His clown face has gone, and a scowl is in its place.

"I was dancing in the rain." My bangs clings to my forehead as I smile at him, but I know charm won't work when he's this angry.

"Your clothes are soaked through."

"But they'll dry."

Ma appears at the end of the tunnel, and she runs to us.

"You'll catch your death," she says, holding out a towel, which she curls around my shoulders.

"I'd best get warm then," I laugh.

"Sorry, Tricks," I hear her say as I dart back toward the costume tent.

Carla has Baby Stan balanced on her lap as she scrubs her face clean.

"What are we going to do with you, Lo?" she says, watching me through her little mirror.

"We should've done the whole performance out in the rain," I say, as I peel back my changeling feathers, careful not to snap them. The white ponytail unclips easy from the back of my head, leaving me shorter-haired again.

"Don't hang your stuff there," Carla says. "You'll have to dry it in Terini."

Baby Stan holds out the hairbrush for me, with his smile that could stop a river.

"Look," I say, as I gently knock the brush against a bottle on the table. "Fairy music."

"Don't be filling his head with your nonsense," she smiles.

"You hear it, don't you?" I whisper close to him, and his laugh floats in wings from him.

RITA

Lo sweeps quickly between the seats, collecting piles of dropped popcorn and ripped tickets. I follow behind her, tipping it all into rubbish bags to tie and throw away. I wonder how many sticky fingers leave their prints on it all. How their skin dust leaves them and becomes a part of us.

"Do you think he watched it?" Lo asks quietly.

"Dean?" I shouldn't even say his name with Ma so close by.

"Who else?" she smiles.

"I'm sure he did."

"Maybe he didn't like it," Lo says. "He didn't stick around." She stops and looks at me. "We could go and find him," she whispers. "It's stopped raining. We can go after we clean up."

"Just us?"

"Yes," she says quietly. "We're old enough. Just us."

I feel torn, because I know we shouldn't, but part of me wants to see her heart shine bright. "OK," I say, before I think any more.

"You will? Even after Newport?" She smiles slightly.

"You won't do that again." In just one night Lo kissed two flattie boys whose names she barely knew. She was sick from drinking when she got home and woke up with her head filled with lightning and regret. Then one came knocking on Terini's door and she hid in the bathroom while I said I didn't know her.

The fountain boy seems different, though. And something about Lo is different too. Something on the edge of her skin lights up when she talks about him.

* * *

We've barely finished cleaning up when we walk off, the candy stripe of our big top growing smaller behind us. Lo's bottle-white hair shines messy in the night's darkness. She'll be cold without a coat, but there's no point in me saying. I've told her that Lil knows more rain is coming, but she might as well not have heard.

"Will Spides and Ash mind that they're not with us?" she asks, linking her arm through mine.

"Maybe," I say. "But I think they'll mind even more that we're looking for a flattie, so I'm not going to tell them."

There are three figures ahead of us, on the edge of our site, lit by one of the street lights.

"He's there," Lo says, without looking at me.

"Are you sure?"

They're standing, all with their hands in their pockets. Two have got their hoods up, almost covering their faces, but the other one turns to us, as though he senses that we're near. It's Lo's boy from the fountain.

"Do we just walk by them?" I ask.

"No. We stop and talk," Lo says.

"What if they're waiting for someone else?"

She looks at me. "He's waiting for me," she says. It's there, in her eyes, and it makes me feel I've made a mistake. We shouldn't have come.

The fountain boy raises his hand and waves at us, at Lo.

"I think maybe Ash and Spider should be here," I say, slowing down so much that I'm barely moving. Lo doesn't stop; she unhooks her arm from mine and just looks back at me and smiles.

"They're fine, Rita," she says. "They're good ones."

"How do you know?" I'm walking to catch up with her, because she can't go on her own.

"I just do."

"Hey," Dean says as we get close.

"Hey back," Lo smiles. A strange silence sits in the middle of us all. The boys in hoods look at us as though we're from a different land. Maybe we are. Maybe they are.

"We watched your show," Dean tells Lo.

"What did you think?" She's all jutting elbows, hands resting on hips.

"It was good."

"Just good?" she smiles.

"Better than good."

One of the boys pulls back his hood, even though Lil's rain is starting to spit. He's the one with his skin scalded from too many spots, and he looks straight at me.

"Don't you get jealous that your sister is the star of the show?"

"I'm not." Lo has anger in her voice. "We're all equal." The boy puts his palms up, as though stopping her.

"No offence meant." And I think he means it. "Anyway, I thought the motorbike bit was the best," he says.

"Typical flattie," Lo mumbles.

"What's a flattie?" the boy asks.

"One of you. Not one of us. Do you know that Rita nearly died when we practiced that?" Lo exaggerates.

"I'm not surprised," he says casually, but he looks impressed. Strange that the closer we come to death, the more they like it.

"What happened?" Dean asks.

"I misjudged my jump," Lo says.

"It could easily have been my mistake," I say. I don't like the guilt that still sits in her.

"Does it really come down to that?" Dean asks. "Just a split-second mistake between you and death?"

"It's the same for us all," Lo says. "Every day you walk the line between dying and surviving too. It's not just us."

The boy with the hood still covering his face nods, his hands still in his pockets, staring hard at the ground.

"You're pretty bendy," the boy with the crumpled skin says.

"Will." Dean sounds annoyed.

"What? They are."

"Do you get scared?" Dean looks at both of us, but I know he's asking Lo. "When you're up high? That you're going to fall?"

"No. Never," Lo says. And I know it's the truth, because it's the same as I feel. "But I have nerves. That's different."

"How?" Dean asks.

"Being nervous keeps you aware," Lo says. "It brightens everything around you, so that you notice it all. Being scared just burns everything, so nothing is clear."

"Burns everything?" Will asks.

"Fries the edges of everything," Lo says. "So you can't see clearly anymore."

"Sounds a bit nuts to me," the boy in the hood says.

"No," Dean interrupts him. "I get it."

"You would." The boy in the hood half laughs. I recognize him now—he was at the fountain too.

The rain is getting heavier, enough to wet our faces and make our hair cold.

"I like the sound of it," Will says. "Frying edges." And he walks to the middle of the road and sits down.

"What are you doing?" Dean asks, looking around.

"Getting scared," Will shouts, lying his whole body flat on the ground.

"You're being an idiot," Dean says.

"I want to see things burning." Will stares up at the black sky, blinking hard into the raindrops.

"I didn't mean it like that," Lo says. She's confused, and it makes her shoot anger at the boy.

"He knows that," I tell her. He's just acting up because he's a flattie who can.

"A car's coming," the boy in the hood says. He's taken his hands from his pockets as he stares deep down the road.

We can all hear it now, the drumming of wheels on tarmac, getting bigger and wider. It sounds larger than a car.

"Get up," Dean says, but Will just lies there.

"I'm getting hotter," he laughs.

"You're not," I tell him. He's a fool, tapping into the wrong side of danger.

It's a van, on the opposite side of the road to us, but with no space to go past Will.

"Get up," Dean says loudly.

The van must see the figure lying down, but it doesn't slow. Instead its horn is pressed and blares toward us. It seems to speed up as it comes and Will lies flat. None of us move. We watch the van swerve, missing Will by just inches. It crashes its wheels up across the pavement, fumes filling the air. The driver screams at us from behind the glass, before the van thuds back onto the road, all noise and lights and anger until it disappears and leaves us all staring at this boy in the road.

He jumps up in one movement and hollers like some sort of wolf.

"Burn baby burn," he shouts, walking back toward us.

"You're an idiot," Dean says, turning away from him and looking straight at Lo. "Sorry about him."

"We're going," I say, pulling on Lo's arm. But even now

she's hesitating, and I know she wants to split herself in two so she can come with me away from Will but also stay talking to her fountain boy in the rain.

"Can I see you again?" Dean asks, and Will smirks and thumps him light on his arm.

Lo looks up at Dean, shielding her eyes from the streaks falling from the wet sky.

"You will," she says. And I know I have to get her away from here, before her heart gets too entangled with his.

"We're going," I say, and I pull her with me, giving her no choice. I make her run from him, heading toward our circle of vans sitting tight against the rain.

The light in Mada is on, so we go up the steps, push open the door, and stamp our wet feet on the mat.

"You're not coming in like that," Ma says, getting up.

Ernest and Spider are sitting with Dad at the table, each holding a fan of cards.

"We're fine, Ma," Lo says, but we wait as she gets a towel and makes us rub through our hair and wipe dry our hands.

"Where did you go?" Spider asks, as Lo and I take off our shoes and put them neatly in the small shoe rack. "Ash and I were looking for you."

"We just went for a walk," I say, saving Lo from a lie she won't want to tell.

"Where's Gramps?" Lo asks, squeezing in beside Spider.

"In bed already trying to sleep, so no party noise from you," Dad tells her. He puts his arm around Ma as she sits back next to him.

"I'm tired in any case," Lo says.

"Not too tired to disrupt a card game I see," Ma smiles at her.

"Did you meet anyone?" Ernest asks.

"No one interesting," I say. I glance quickly at Lo so she doesn't say more. "Why's Rob not playing?"

"He chose to turn in early," Dad says, his fingers flicking quick through his cards. "It's your turn." He nods at Ernest.

"I'd get rid of that ace of clubs when it's your go, Spider," Lo says laughing. Spider opens his mouth like a goldfish and holds his cards away from her.

"Don't spoil it, Lo," Ma tells her.

"I'm here to help," she says.

"You're here to be a pest," Dad says, but his frown is lined with a smile.

"Do you want one of these?" Ma asks, passing the plate of bread twists to me. The stringy dough we plaited together this afternoon is solid and cracked brown where we painted it with egg yolk.

"Needs cheese, I'm thinking," Spider says, grabbing another when he's barely finished chewing his own.

"You can keep your thinkings," Lo says, even though she didn't help us make them.

"I'm out," Dad says, laying his fan of cards flat on the table. "Three sixes and a run of hearts." He's so proud of winning, his dad smile wide.

"That's not fair," Ernest says. "I was so close."

"It's all fair," Dad chuckles. Fair is a word that was invented for him. The cards look small in his hands as he sweeps them all up, packs them neat and shuffles them. "Who's in?"

"I'm going to bed," Lo says, yawning and putting her arms up high as though she needs to prove it to us.

"I could do with an early night too," I say.

"Bed already?" Ma asks.

"I suppose so," Lo says, and we get up together, like twins from the womb. I lean over to kiss Dad. My mom sweeps her fingers over her forehead before touching my own, passing her good dreams to me.

"Sweet dreams," she says as she does the same to Lo.

My shoes feel cold as I put them on, Lo holding my arm to stop herself from toppling.

"Night all," she says, before we close the door on them.

I'd forgotten about the rain. It's not too strong, but it's reminding us it's there. Lo runs to Terini, jumps up the steps and unlocks our door. She holds it open to me, with one arm behind her.

"I won't be long," I say. I know she's confused. "I just need to see someone." I'm walking away, so that she can't ask too many questions and I won't have to lie.

"Ash?" she asks.

I wave my hand at her. "Don't worry," I say. "I'll be back soon." And I run quickly around the edge of the big top so that she can no longer see me.

Chapter Three

LO

The rain is drying, but the morning sky is still gray as I walk back toward our van.

"Lo, come and see this." Spider appears from the side of the big top and grabs my hand.

"What?" But he puts his fingers to shush my lips, and I let him pull me through new puddles that float our sawdust on their surface.

We run around the edge of the tent, until we're outside Rob's van. Spider crouches low, and I copy him.

"What is it?" I mouth.

"Look." And he points to the window above us. I hesitate. Rob would kill me if he saw me looking in his van.

I don't know what I expect to see through the crack in the curtain, but it isn't this. In the grim light of his van, Rob is naked on his bed.

I duck down and screw my face up at Spider.

"Why would I want to see that?" I ask.

Spider looks suddenly awkward. "I thought it was funny."

"Who's he with?" I ask.

Spider's face sparks into life again. "I don't know."

Slowly, he slides up toward the window. I'm not sure our luck will last. If Rob sees him, the heavens will fall.

Something crosses over Spider's face, before he crouches quickly down again.

"Who is it?" I ask.

"I couldn't see," he answers. "Let's go."

"You did see."

"I didn't. It's too dark in there. Let's go."

He takes my hand, so I have no choice but to be led away.

I try to leave the image of Rob behind, but it trails along beside us.

"Who was he with, Spider?" I ask again, when we're far enough from the van to stop walking and to talk without whispering.

"I said I didn't see, so I didn't."

"I know a lie when I hear one," I tell him.

"I wouldn't lie to you, Lo," he says earnestly, ripping honesty in two.

"Lo." Spider grabs my hand.

"I want to see who it was." I pull myself free and start walking back.

Spider is beside me. "It's too dark. You won't be able to."

"You saw."

"I didn't." He squeezes in another lie. "It's no business of ours. You can't go spying on people."

"You brought me here in the first place."

"I thought it would be funny." His voice is quiet as we get close. I stand to the side of the window.

"Lo," Spider whispers.

Through the line of glass I see Rob turned away from us. Next to him is my mom, standing by the bed, pulling her shirt over her bare arms.

Spider drags me back.

"You saw?" he asks, but I can only stare at him.

He's holding my hand, and we're walking over a ground that feels split in two. The air is too thick, and I make him stop.

"My mom."

"I know." He shakes his head, as though trying to loosen the image and let it drop away.

"Did I see it wrong?" I ask.

"I don't think so."

I watch my feet step on the grass. I need to rewind time.

I need to have not seen it. Because if I haven't seen it, maybe it hasn't happened. It could erase, so it never existed.

"My dad," I say. The words are attached to so many others.

I think I should be crying, but I'm blocked up by a feeling I've never felt before. It's like anger, but it's bubbled tight onto something else that wants to pop and spill inside me.

Spider keeps hold of my hand as he leads me away and across the open park. The wall he finds for us to sit on is low and backed by a single line of trees, before the road.

We look back toward our vans. They're different now, smudged with something that wants to push them flat. Our big top stands red and yellow in the middle, the center of it poking too high toward the sky.

"How can I ever look at her again?" I ask finally.

"She's your mom."

"Not the mom I thought she was." It suddenly feels like

my family has thick dirt on them, but my mom used to shine like stars.

"You don't know all the story," Spider says.

"My parents being together is the story."

"Do you think he knows?" Spider asks.

My dad, sitting at the table, his arm around our mom.

"No," I say.

Spider spits on the ground.

"I hate Rob," I say, but the words hurt.

"Will you tell Rita?" Spider asks.

"I won't tell anyone," I say. "It'll kill my dad if he finds out." I look up at Spider, more earnestly than I ever have. "And you mustn't too. Promise me, Spider."

He looks lost. I know he wishes he hadn't seen it either.

"I promise," he says.

The air is solid, and I don't like the way it makes me breathe. But we walk back through it, back to a world that's shifted, and I no longer know where I fit.

Spider leaves me near Terini. I watch as he walks away, and then, instead of going up the steps as I should, I turn and start to walk out of the park.

If anyone sees me, no one says. No one shouts my name. I make it look like I've got a purpose, my steps stronger than I feel.

Our vans all have their backs to me as I head for the rush of cars. I follow their stream and stop for the light and cross the road we walked up two nights ago, when my life was whole.

The gray shops are open now, sucking in and spitting out shoppers. The fountain is here. I should have left the coin sunk at the bottom. It's brought the wrong luck, the bad kind that whips your eyes to make you see.

The child touching the spray is what makes me cry. His

mom holding his hand, keeping him safe. I walk on past and wipe my eyes on my sleeve. My mom was meant to keep holding our hands, not be the one to throw us to the lions.

The shops end abruptly, replaced by a merry-go-round with horses that creak up and down in endless circles. A girl looks up as I cry. She doesn't mind that she stares at me.

Then houses. Lots of them, that let me walk alongside them and don't even pretend to look away from the girl in the broken circus.

"Hey!" I can't see where the voice is coming from. "Laura."

I turn and it's him. Dean from the fountain, and he's running toward me.

"Are you OK?" he asks. I just look at him. "I saw you from the window. That's my house." He points back down the street.

"I'm just looking around," I say. But he must know that something is wrong as I cough and wipe my eyes.

"I can show you," he says.

"Show me what?"

"Around." He smiles. And it's there, despite my world disappearing, there's that feeling in my bones. A spark I want to light to see where it leads me.

"OK."

We walk together, away from the merry-go-round, away from the fountain and the park with our tents and my mom in Rob's van pulling her shirt over her naked arms.

"Where are your friends?" I ask.

"They're at college."

"You're not?"

"Not until this afternoon."

At the end of the street, we turn into another, with more houses.

"Where's your sister?" he asks.

"At the site, getting ready for later. As I should be."

"You have a show today?"

"Two."

We walk with our arms almost touching.

"Did you have a fight with her?" He looks at me and my mind tumbles.

"No. We rarely fight."

But now there'll be unspoken words drawing a big, dark line between us. I want to unpick it, to scrub it out, but it's there, waiting to divide us.

"I liked your show," he says, awkward for something to say. I can feel that he's looking at me again, but I keep my eyes on the pavement that quietly takes my feet.

"Thanks." I should say more, but all I can think of is Rob and Ma in that van. How her red lips and careful hair now make too much sense. When did the hoop earrings appear? Weeks? Months? How long ago did we lose her without knowing? How long has Rob been the extra person in our van, who we couldn't see?

Dean cuts down a thin alley, and I follow him. The bricks of houses either side hold us in. The air doesn't move. It feels stuck with the breath of every person who ever walked down here. I share it with the ghosts of shuffling old men and running children.

At the end, there's a big, broken building with rows and rows of windows, going up and across. Every single one has been smashed through.

"My mom used to work here," Dean says.

Our feet crunch on loose stones as he leads me around to the side. Dean climbs up onto an old bin and pulls himself on top of a rusting blue container. Without asking if I want to, he stands up and puts out his hand for me. And I go, up toward him, letting him help me until we're standing together on the rickety metal.

The window in front of us is empty of glass and Dean climbs through.

"Careful," he says, reaching back to help me balance. On this side, in here, I'm alone with him.

"This way."

We walk together across the big room, its ceiling too low. The door at the end is open.

"It was a soap factory," Dean says. "You wouldn't believe this place once kept the world clean."

The air holds memories I can almost touch.

"I wasn't born when she worked here," Dean tells me as we walk together up the stairs. "I like to imagine it, what she was like." His mother's younger self runs past us. Her face is like his, and she looks at me and smiles before she disappears.

"Where does she work now?" I ask.

"In the supermarket bakery in the mornings and then as a cleaner."

"Was she happier here?"

"I like to think so." I can see unspoken thoughts on his face. I wait for them to leave him and trickle into the walls to find her ghost.

"How many stairs?" I ask as we turn to see more going up.

"A few more."

There're too many, and there's too much time to think about my dad, about the hurt waiting around the corner for him. I try instead to smell the flecks of soap hidden in the dust.

At the top, there's a metal ladder fixed to the wall.

"It should be easy for you," he says, and he's right. I climb ladders in my sleep. "I'll go first to unhook the latch."

I can tell he's been here a hundred times. He pushes back the flat door at the top and lets the white sky come tumbling in.

I hold the metal rungs and go up through the hole that leads to the roof.

"Look," he says. And I do, and I see over the houses and streets to a patch of green scattered with tiny white vans and the red and yellow of our big top so small that I could pick it up with my fingers.

"Do you like it?" he asks.

"Yes." I've never seen so far.

The roof is flat, with catches of puddles that haven't dried. There's no barrier at the edge, and I want to walk there, have my feet touch where the solid line meets the air.

"There's my house." Dean points toward the street we just walked down. "The one with the red door." Miniature buildings waiting patiently. I try to imagine the quiet. The stillness. The never moving on.

"What's it like?" I ask. "Living somewhere permanently?"

"It's good, I suppose."

"Who do you live with?"

"Just my mom."

"Just your mom?" In my life there's family around every corner, there's noise and color so bright it suffocates at times. "Where's your dad?"

Dean raises his shoulders awkward. "I don't have one."

"Did he die?" Although I'm scared to ask.

"No. I just never knew him." He speaks like he doesn't care, but I can see he's unsettled behind his eyes. "He stayed for about a year after I was born. There one day, gone the next."

"He didn't keep in touch?"

"No."

I think of our dad, keeping us safe on his shoulders above any storm.

"Do you have sisters or brothers?" I ask, trying to make it OK again for Dean. And needing to block out thoughts of Ma's betrayal striking into my dad.

"I've got a brother who comes to visit sometimes, but he doesn't live with us anymore."

"So there are empty bedrooms?"

"No. We used to share our room."

"It must be very quiet, just you and your mom."

"It just feels normal to us."

Normal. My normal has turned to dust. I look at his eyes, wondering whether I can trust him.

"I saw my mom in a friend's van," I say quickly. "Where she shouldn't have been. Spider showed me."

Dean looks at me, waiting for the words to settle.

"It was Rob's van," I carry on. "He joined our circus a few years ago. He's meant to be family."

"And they were together?"

"Yes."

"When did you see it?"

"Just now." I want answers from him, on how to put it all right.

"Did you suspect?"

"No. I never thought she'd do this. I never thought Rob would."

"How come he's in your circus?"

"He wanted to join and he was good enough."

"That simple?"

"He trained as a dancer but wanted something different. Tricks says if it wasn't for Rob, our circus might not've survived. He made us change, so more people came to see us." But the memory of his naked back burns into me.

Dean puts his hands into the pockets of his jeans as he looks at me.

"What's he like?"

"He's just Rob." I remember him turning up and asking to audition. Spider, Rita, and I sat and watched. He was beautiful, lost in his dance. And he brought with him pinches of stories from his life that had stood still.

But he also brought this.

"I'm worried that my dad is going to hurt." Anger creeps up through the roof we're standing on, through my shoes, seeping into my skin.

"Are you going to tell your mom? What you saw?"

I imagine it. I see myself walking up the steps of Mada and making her look at me, and I'll tell her I saw Rob's skin on hers.

"If I do, my dad will definitely find out." I could reach up now and touch the sky with my fingertips. Pull myself through the blue away from all of this. "I have to go back and pretend I know nothing," I say flatly.

"Will your friend tell anyone?"

"Spider? No, he promised he won't." And to him she was my mom who could do no wrong.

"Is Spider your boyfriend?" Dean is looking at me again and it makes my anger change into something else.

"No."

"And you're not interested in him?"

"No." I can't explain to him how Spider would never want to be with me. How people wait for us to be together, but

Spider has secrets, and I know we never will.

Dean nods and I don't know if his smile is for me, or for the air that holds the tiny houses below us.

"This is where I come to think," Dean says. "You can come back if you want. If you need to."

"I'd like that," I say, because I would. Up here, I feel like a bird, that I could fly anywhere.

"I could take you there, too, if you'd like." Dean points to a ribbon of river beyond the houses, just past where the fields start. "It's a good place."

"Healing water?"

"Maybe." He smiles. We could sit together by the stream.

"Are you at college a lot?" I ask.

"A fair bit."

"Do you like it?"

"It's all right."

"I can't imagine going to the same place all the time."

Dean pauses and looks at me. "Do you really like the moving on? Don't you ever want to stop and set up home?"

"I have a home," I say, but inside I'm hesitating.

"But put down roots. Be in one place?"

"I don't think I could. I'd be scared I'd fall off."

"Fall off what?"

"The edge of the world," I say. "I know it doesn't make sense, but it's how I feel."

"Then it does make sense," Dean says. I look at him and wonder how he knows. How a flattie can understand. Maybe I could tell him how sometimes I do feel trapped by our moving wheels, tied tight to them, and I want to see what would happen if I cut myself free.

"I'm going to have to go back," is all I say and Dean nods.

"Can I come and see you?"

Dean, walking into our site, up Terini's steps.

"Dad wouldn't be too welcoming," I tell him.

"If you introduce me, he'd know I'm nice." He smiles, but he doesn't understand.

"He'd never let me get involved with a flattie."

"Never?"

"No."

The word sounds like a final bell, hanging heavy on its own. I can tell by Dean's eyes that he doesn't hear it.

"Can I take your number then?" he asks.

"My number?"

"Of your phone."

"I don't have one," I say.

"You don't have a phone?"

"What'd be the point? I live with everyone I'd want to phone."

"Except for me." He smiles at me again, and I feel myself turn my back on Dad's wishes.

"Except for you." I look at him. "I'll come and find you again." I know we have to go, but I wait for a second and breathe in the space of the birds, of their feathers, their wings. Their freedom trickles down inside me and settles on the walls of my lungs. Then I walk to the edge of the hole in the roof, balance on one leg, pressing my foot hard down.

"What are you doing?" Dean asks.

"I'm leaving my footprint," I say. "Rita and I always do, wherever we go, so we know we've been there. And the place remembers that we were there too."

Dean watches me, smiling, before I step over the ledge and slide easily down the ladder.

Chapter Four

LO

I stand on the wooden platform, my feet waiting at the edge. I know if I look down I'll see the faces bent up toward us, that same expression swept across them all as our music makes their hearts beat faster.

Rita swings, her smile fixed. The timing has to be right, but we have it ticking in our blood, and we never make mistakes on this. She spins and hooks her knees over her trapeze, arms stretched down to the floor far below.

I jump. She grabs my wrists and I hold her tight. We keep our line straight, and I know that the air has changed as the people watching will have stopped their breaths.

The wind is sharp past my skin as I twist my body bent and Rita holds my ankles, so my arms are free to catch the trapeze that Ash pushes toward me. I reach and my powdered hands hold the sturdy bar. The muscles in my arms tense, as I spin myself through and up so that I'm sitting, swinging high, pulling on the ropes.

We're meant to somersault in time together, but suddenly I'm standing on my trapeze. I look at Rita, silently telling her to trust me, that I won't fall. I move so that I'm on tiptoes on the bar, lifting one leg to stretch out behind. I'm an angel, flying, and it's dangerous, so Rob should be proud. And if I fall, it'll all be his fault.

For a brief second, I let go. I feel gravity and luck hold me in their palm, hold the changeling by the tips of her wings, between her two worlds. Everything stops. It's just me and my heartbeat, before noise crashes back in and I grab the ropes again.

If Tricks has seen, he'll be furious. Never go off script. Never, ever on the trapeze. But I feel bulletproof.

I crook my knees over the bar and swing down again. I move faster until I can let go and somersault, knowing Rita will catch me. Soon, Tricks says, I'll be ready for the blackout. In a few months' time, they'll put a hood over me and I'll flip blind from the trapeze, with Rita to grab me safe.

I swing back onto the ledge. Opposite each other, Rita and I wave to the crowd below. Sometimes, when I walk down the ladder, I let the cheering seep right into me. Today, I keep it at the edge of my skin.

* * *

It always feels cramped in the costume tent. Ma is sitting facing the mirror, twisting her curls high onto her head. She's supposed to be a grieving mother, searching for her lost child, but she's putting more make-up on her already thickly made-up face.

"It's busy tonight," she says.

"Why wouldn't it be?" I reply, taking the feathers from my hair.

"I thought it might not be, because you said it was a strange town." She pauses, looking confused.

"I never said that."

I take the gold feather headdress from the shelf and start to fix it roughly across my forehead, clipping it tight behind my ears.

"Has Spider upset you?" she asks.

"No." I don't want to be in here, with the lies between us choking up my throat.

"Well, whatever it is, it's never as bad as it seems," she says, standing up. She leans down to kiss my cheek as she passes.

When she's gone, I wipe away where her lips were.

"What's wrong, Lo?" Rita asks. She stands next to me, but I won't look her in the eye.

"I just don't feel like performing tonight," I say.

"You have to do the rest of the show," she says.

"I know."

I'll find my smile. I'll push Rob's van away. I'll try to piece my mom's skin back together again.

"Where did you go earlier?" Rita asks.

"I was looking around," I say.

"You never look around on your own." I can tell she's put out. "Especially in such a gray town."

"I met that boy. Dean." I'll risk this secret with her, to keep the other one safe.

"Where?"

"I was walking and he saw me."

"Lo." She looks serious. "You can't go falling in love with a flattie."

"I don't love him. I only spoke to him."

"I can tell by your eyes what you're thinking."

"Then will you help me see him again?" I ask her.

"Lo."

"We won't get caught."

"It's not that."

"It'll only be for a bit. I just want to talk to him, and then when we move on I probably won't see him again."

I see the thoughts jarring fast in her.

"OK," she finally says.

"You will?"

"Yes."

"You're brilliant, Rita." And I hug her tight and mean every inch of it. Because I know that she's helping me cross a line that to her is more dangerous than flying between burning wires.

★ ★ ★

"I'm not really encouraging this," Rita says. But she's with me all the same, walking quietly across the park, grass under our feet and star-shine above our heads. "I'm only doing it to cheer you up."

"I'm not sad," I tell her.

"Something's wrong." She doesn't ask any more. She knows I tell her everything when I find the words. But this time, she can't see the crack in the earth between us. She doesn't know that I have to step away from her, before I tumble in.

We cross at the traffic lights, her arm in mine.

"It doesn't get any prettier," she says, as we walk between the lines of shops.

The fountain is empty of people.

"He's not here," Rita says, and I can sense relief folding into her words.

"He didn't say he would be."

The water splashes down, but this time I don't touch it.

"It'd be dangerous, Lo, to like him."

We sit on the fountain's stone ledge, our backs to the money spun down under the wet.

"You'd get hurt," she says. "They're not like us."

"But maybe I don't want to be with one of ours." I expect that she'll be shocked, but she only looks at me calmly.

"That'll change. You'll change."

"So you're happy with Ash again now?"

Rita shrugs, but I can see confusion still sitting awkward in her eyes. "Spider will grow up, and you'll fall for him when you're least expecting it," is all she says.

I look at her with her curls half clipped up, her eyes rimmed in black, and I wonder if she really can't see what I do, how Spider will never love me, not in that way.

"Will it really all be enough for you?" I ask.

"All of what?"

"The life we've got."

She looks confused, as though she's never really thought that there could be something else, that an alternative does exist.

"We've got a good life, Lo."

"I know." Because we do. We did. The stone seat beneath us is cold.

"Dean's not coming, is he?" I ask.

"I don't think so."

Maybe he's sitting on the roof, watching the lights of the town.

"Let's go." I stand up and put my hand out for my sister. She takes it and we walk back together, toward our home that our mom has set adrift.

We stop by Mada to say goodnight, as we always do, but Dad sits alone on the sofa. He only has the lamp on, and it shines too small a light on his book.

"You'll damage your eyes," Rita scolds him, flicking on the main light. He smiles at us, though it seems to take a few seconds for him to realize that we're really here.

Gramps sits silently in the corner. He doesn't even rock his chair.

"Where's Ma?" I ask, before I've time to wish I hadn't.

"In bed," Dad says and relief grabs me quick.

Maybe their meeting of skins was just that. Maybe it's never happened before and it never will again.

But it hurts me now to see my dad, his hair that never combs straight, the crease of his collar almost flat to his neck. My dad, whose eyes are open, but he just can't see.

"Night, Gramps," Rita says, curling in to hug him.

"Night, love."

And as I hug him too, he squeezes my shoulder gently and I know that's enough.

I kiss my dad and try to smell my mom on him. But there's just him—the rumble of his skin, the smoke from his yellow-tipped fingers. I can't find her anywhere.

RITA

"I'm not ready for bed yet," Lo says, as we leave Dad reading in his silent room. I can tell she's restless, energy still buzzing in her blood. "Let's go to Spider's." She points to where the light is on in his van, but the curtains are closed.

"He might be sleeping," I say.

"He won't be," Lo says. We walk up the steps and she pushes open his door that he always leaves unlocked. Ash, Spider and Rob sit huddled at the table, the bed hooked back neatly on the wall. Lo hesitates and doesn't go in.

"You can come and bring some sense to this," Ash tells us. He's already moving up to make room, but Lo still doesn't move.

"It's OK," Spider tells her and she steps inside. It smells so strong of boys in here, their skin and their sprays. It's a different world from Terini.

The bench is too small for all of us, so Lo sits on Spider's lap. There's something about her that needs him there tonight. I sit down next to Rob. I feel his arm against mine.

"How's your injury?" Rob asks as he touches my shoulder.

"Much better." I can't help breathing in as I say the words.

"Rob is still dreaming up new ways to kill us," Ash says. He doesn't notice this new feeling around me when I'm with Rob. Maybe I'm imagining it all.

"No one is going to die," Rob says, rubbing the top of his arm with his palm. "But if they want danger, then we have to give them danger."

"Even after what happened to Rita?" Ash asks.

"I won't let Rita get hurt again." Rob looks at me. I don't look away, even when he turns back to the others.

"Are you going to tell them what you're planning, then?" Spider asks.

"Is this your ma's shortbread?" Lo interrupts, picking up a crumbling slab from the plate and putting the whole thing in her mouth.

"None other," Spider says. Ash passes me one, and I don't know why I hesitate before I take it.

"Escapology," Rob says. He bites into his shortbread and licks a crumb from his thumb.

"What's that?" I ask.

"When someone is strapped in somewhere, like in a burning suit, and they have to escape in a certain amount of time. The audience'll love it."

"But none of us can do it," Spider tells him.

"You'll learn," Rob says. "You lot can do anything you put your mind to."

Lo does a strange laugh and looks only at the wall.

"Your parents will definitely be interested," I tell Spider. "I think it's a good idea."

"So I've got at least one on my side," Rob smiles at me.

"I'm not convinced." Ash turns his mouth up like a stubborn child. "I've got to think about Sarah too. What if you decide to lock her in some box and we can't get her out?"

"You're being a bit dramatic." Rob's authority turns Ash's words small.

"Maybe Ash just cares about what happens to us," Lo says sharply.

"I care as much as anyone," Rob says. "I might have started off as a flattie, but I'm part of you all now."

68

"I can't listen to any more of this." The anger of Lo's voice shocks us all. "I'm going to bed."

"Yeah," Ash says. "I'm tired. I think that's me done too." He stands up and our unit breaks. "Shall I walk you back to Terini, Rita?" He holds out his hand to me, but I don't take it.

"I'm going to stay here for a bit," I say. The disappointment in his face is habit to him now, part of the game we play.

"Tomorrow?"

"Maybe."

I think he might bend down and kiss me, but he doesn't.

"You tease him too much, Rita," Rob laughs. "One day he might just give up trying."

"Do you know, I think I need my van back now. I need to go to bed too," Spider says. His yawn is exaggerated, his tiredness out of nowhere. Rob looks put out. He has ideas that will save us and no one wants to listen.

"I can come to yours, Rob," I say. "If you want to talk about your ideas more."

"No," Lo interrupts. "Dad will kill you if you're too tired for the performance tomorrow."

"It's not that late." She's annoyed me now, speaking as though she's the eldest.

"It's OK. Lo's right," Rob says. "Another time, Rita?"

"That'd be good," I say.

And I get up to follow Lo out of the door, but she's already gone.

LO

"What's wrong, Lo?" Rita asks, as she hangs her jeans neat in our cupboard. I can't find the words to answer her, so I just lie in bed, staring at the slats of her top bunk. "Is it because Dean wasn't at the fountain?" She puts her feet on the ladder, just the one step she touches before she pulls herself up. Witches wait on the other rungs, so she won't let her feet near them. She turns off the light, and everything goes black. "Or don't you like Rob's new ideas?"

She's brought him in here, when I want to forget.

"It's not that."

"He won't do anything that would hurt us." I hear her turn over and know she pulls her duvet soft around her shoulder.

"I'm scared about Gramps dying," I say, to push Rob away from the room.

"Gramps isn't going anywhere," she says.

"He will, though. Someday, he won't be here."

"Not for ages, Lo."

"How do you know that? He's getting older every day."

"So are we all."

"You know what I mean."

"Don't, Lo."

"I'm scared that Gramps's words are running out," I whisper. "That he's used most of them up."

There's a silence, but I know she thinks and breathes.

"I wonder where our last ones go?" I say.

"Our words?"

"Yes. Our very last ones. I wonder if they collect somewhere."

"Imagine if every word we ever said was stored some-place," Rita says. "It'd be very loud."

"It'd be like white noise. Just a blur, where you can't work them out."

"Maybe," Rita says.

"If you put all our words we've ever spoken and laid them end to end on the ground, how many times around the world would they go?"

"Night, Lo," Rita says.

"Don't you want to work it out?"

She laughs lightly, and I know sleep is already reaching out for her.

"I'm going to work it all out from the beginning," I say. "From the very first word."

"You remember them all?"

"Yes."

"Liar." And she laughs again as I close my eyes.

But today's words won't lie flat. They lift like steam, impossible to hold. Maybe they're better that way. If I can change my mom and Rob being together into only words and let them drift up through my fingers, maybe I can let them go. Imagine they were never here.

But anger is twisting me in waves. I stare into the blackness, reaching up to touch the slats of Rita's bed to try to still me. I feel so small, too small to cope with all of this.

I can't tell her Ma's secret that has turned me inside out and will do the same to my dad. Because if Rita knew the truth, her skin would disappear.

The air in here is too small and I think I'll be sick, so I push back my duvet and stumble from our room into the dark bathroom. I clutch the edge of the toilet until I'm sure it'll break.

Hold it so tight, because Rob has taken our gravity and I'm afraid we'll all fall.

Him naked with my mom.

The stars collide and crack as I lie on the floor, and I have to twist close to the sink so that I can feel its cold. I wait for the anger to roll away. Imagine it as a ball of red in an empty field. It's bigger than me, but I'm strong enough, and I push it until it moves. And I push it again and watch as it starts to go faster from me, getting smaller and smaller until I think it'll disappear.

I stand up and unlock the door.

"Lo?" Rita is standing here, her forehead knotted with confusion. "What's wrong?"

But I don't want the anger to come crashing back. "Nothing," I say, the word weighted with lies. And I don't give her a chance to say more as I walk quickly past her and slide deep into my bed.

★ ★ ★

At breakfast, I watch my mom for clues, but she doesn't give any away. She's quiet as we eat our bacon in bread. There's something, though. She's got smiles inside her that she's not letting out.

"Shall we go to the town later?" I ask Rita. I try to sound casual, as though there's not someone I want to see.

"I thought it was too quiet," my dad says. "That there wasn't much there." He's grisly this morning, as though ulcers are gnawing at his gums again.

"It's not so bad," I say.

The smell of the fried bacon clings to the tablecloth, to

the walls. It's the one meal that Ma likes to keep the windows closed for. She says the smell makes the eating twice as good.

Ma puts a poached egg on my plate. She's cooked it just how I like it, so the white is set, but the yolk pops and soaks around it.

"Thank you," I say, trying not to see those hoop earrings, or her hair twisted up beautiful when the day is only just beginning.

Instead I stare at the faded flower pattern in the curtain and wind myself tight into the material, so no one can see my thoughts.

Rita piles her egg between her bread, pressing on it until the yellow runs down the side. Gramps is waiting patiently for Ma to drip his soft bread into the frying fat. His unread book sits open on his lap.

"I'll be glad to see the back of it," Ma says. "It's a strange place."

"You've hardly seen any of it," I snap at her. Rita looks shocked at my spikiness.

"Don't be rude to your mother," Dad says.

I want to say more. I want to say so, so much more. But instead, I spill silent words into the bacon I'm chewing and wash it down with a mouthful of orange juice that tastes too bitter.

We clean the dishes together, Rita and I. I have to keep shaking my wrist into the air to stop my bracelets from dunking in the suds.

"Rob's teaching me bridge today," Rita says.

I watch the air to see if it ripples around my mom, but it stays completely still.

"Bridge?" I say. "That's for old people."

"Rob says it's not," Rita says. "It takes brains and a lot of skill."

"You'll be useless, then," I say.

"I can always rely on you for love, Lo."

"Do you want more tea, Gramps?" Ma asks.

At first he doesn't look at her, but when he does, I wonder if somehow he knows. Somehow he can sense another man in our home.

I put down my cloth, pick up my jacket and just leave them all. I can't stand to be breathing Rob's breath where it shouldn't be.

"Lo?" I hear Ma ask, but I close her off with the front door of their van and leave her jangled dirt where I can't see it.

I know where I'm going, but I pretend to myself that I don't, as I cross the park and the road. The streets are busier today, but no one notices the girl from the circus walking among them in the trickling rain. No one knows that there's a line of hurt too deep and painful in my heart and Dean seems to be the only person who can take it away.

The fountain has so many people around it I can barely see its water. I slow down, but none of them are Dean.

The merry-go-round has come alive, the horses running in their endless circle, children kicking their legs against the lifeless bodies. I hold its music to me as I walk away.

I'm on Dean's street. It's strange to think that a few days ago I never knew it existed, but now my heart thumps too quick at the sight of it. I slow down, glancing through the windows until I get to the red door. Close up, I see that the paint is peeling and there are weeds peeping between a crack in the steps. Just small ones, but Ma wouldn't approve. Without thinking, I crouch down and pinch the wiry green in my fingers, and it pulls easily from the earth. I'm left standing with it in my hand, so I throw it onto the pavement, where shoes will hopefully kick it into the road.

There are two doorbells by the front door, and I'm unsure which one to press, so instead I knock on the red wood. There's silence on the other side, and I wonder whether I should just turn and run. Yet I don't.

I'm about to knock again when the door opens and Dean is here. He looks surprised and embarrassed and I think I shouldn't have come. But I needed to see him.

"Laura," he says, keeping the door almost closed.

"We're going tomorrow," I say, as though that's a reason to be here, uninvited on his doorstep.

"Already?"

"Yes." I feel the gap between us filling with roads and obstacles and impossibilities. "Can we go for a walk?"

Dean looks over his shoulder. "I'll just get my coat." And he walks down the corridor behind him, through the open door at the end.

The wet air of the street is pushing past me, so I step inside, into a hallway that smells stale and still. There's a small blackboard with a half-smudged message, a piece of blue chalk hanging from a string. On a shelf are two wooden boxes, one with letters lying flat inside. I'd imagined flowers at a table, wallpaper on the walls.

"Dean?"

"I'm ready," he says, coming out, but I want to see his home, I want to know his life.

"Can you show me?" I ask.

"Show you what?"

"Inside."

"It's just a small flat. There's not much to see."

"I've never been in someone's house."

"Never?"

"No."

Dean hesitates, his hand ready to pull the door shut.

"It's not exactly a great example," he says.

I smile up at him. "Please?"

He raises his eyebrows at me. "OK." And I start to take off my shoes before he can change his mind.

"You can keep them on," he says.

"I can?"

"Our floor isn't exactly shiny."

The door opens into another hallway, a box with no windows and doors leading from it. The kitchen next to us is thin but stuffed full with pans and plates and piles of paper. China is stacked crooked in the washing-up bowl.

"I did warn you," he says. "Mom and I aren't the tidiest."

"You need to get our Rita in here. She'd sort you out." I imagine her in this kitchen with a door to shut off the world, three cupboards tacked onto the wall in a row.

"Is that your garden?" I point through the window.

"If you can call it that."

"It's all concrete." I don't want to sound disappointed, but it's just slabs of gray, with two large pots brimmed with empty earth.

"I reckon your garden is better," Dean says.

"I haven't got one."

"You've got all the parks and places where you stop."

"They're not mine. I'd like a proper one, with a vegetable patch, so I could grow tomatoes."

"Fair enough." He smiles at me.

"Where do you eat your meals?"

"On our laps in here." The room next to the kitchen has a sofa piled with clothes. A line of shelves reaches floor to ceiling, crammed with books and magazines falling over themselves.

"Is it different than what you expected?" he asks.

"A bit," I admit. "It's messier." And he laughs, but I don't know how his thoughts even find space, with all this tangled in his mind. "I like the way it feels permanent, though."

"The mess?"

"Your home."

I want to see his bedroom, but I don't ask. Instead, I just stop in the doorway and glance in. His bed is unmade, pushed up against the window looking out on the street. The wall is covered with pictures, some ripped from a sketchbook with pencil lines of trees and roots and leaves, others bigger than us, paintings of skateboards twisting in the sky. They're brilliant and beautiful.

"Did you do these?" I ask.

"Yes." He looks proud and embarrassed all twined together.

"Is that what you do at college?"

"No. Engineering."

"What's that?"

"Designing engines."

"So kind of like art?"

He doesn't look sure. "I suppose."

"Don't you like it?"

"It's what I've got to do." He closes his bedroom door, as if to shut off the conversation. "Ready?"

"Yes." But even with all the mess twisted everywhere, I don't want to leave. I want to take off my shoes and curl up on the sofa, look out on the concrete garden and imagine what I can grow.

I follow Dean from his flat, and he just takes my hand and leads me from this building of bricks, out into the faltering rain.

We walk in silence and I think I should speak, but I don't know what to say. The right words settle but then drift and disappear. The street feels different, now that I've seen inside a part of it. I feel different, as Dean and I walk down the sour-smelling alleyway and out toward the factory.

Dean helps me onto the blue container, and we jump through our shattered window. Inside, he shakes the raindrops from his hair before he looks at me. I feel the world shift.

"It's a bit wet for the roof," he says. And when he smiles, I know it's too late. I know that somehow this boy has got into my blood and I don't want to travel away from him.

He holds my hand again, as though it's the most natural thing in the world. Because maybe it is. Maybe this was always meant to happen. Maybe Rita would say that our souls have known all along that they'd find each other.

We go through the furthest door, the opposite way of the stairs to the roof. The corridor in front of us stretches long and is scattered with broken windows all down one side. When we walk, the shattered glass crunches like tiny bones under our feet.

Through the door at the end and we're in a small room. Dean climbs onto a big metal shelf sticking strangely from the wall and holds down his arm to help me up. I let him, even though I could easily climb it on my own, and we sit together, our legs hanging down, touching slightly.

Opposite us, empty windows face out over fields. The stillness around feels wrong, as though somehow we're cheating.

I move slightly, my feet tapping gently on the shelves, the sound filling the room.

"What's your mom like?" I ask.

"She's good. When I see her. She's out of the house by four in the morning to get to the bakery."

"That's the middle of the night."

"For most people."

There's a sadness in him that makes me scared to take his hand, but I do.

"Do you miss your dad?" I ask.

"There's nothing to miss," he says. "I never really knew him."

"I'm sorry."

"No need to be," he says. "You can't miss what you've never had."

"I think you can."

We sit in silence, and I wonder if I've asked too much, if I've opened some hurt too big for me to understand.

"So you're moving on tomorrow?" Dean eventually says.

"Yes."

Dean nods, looking at me. We're silent, our thoughts meeting, and I wonder if they're the same.

"Shall we go to the river?" He points to the twisting line in the distance that breaks up the fields.

"Now?" I ask this boy I barely know. This boy who shares my secret.

"If you'd like."

I almost laugh, but I don't know why. "OK," I say, and he jumps down and reaches out to help me.

We leave the factory at our backs, the air clean of rain as we walk down new streets with houses held close together. We have to cross a road with so many cars, before we run up a steep bank to see fields on the other side. It's a different world, green after all the gray and the sound has changed.

"This way," Dean says.

The grass is damp against my ankles. Above us, two birds fly together, dipping close before they disappear their separate ways. We climb a fence and walk to where the river quietly makes its way through the fields. I want to put my thoughts of Ma and Rob on a raft and watch them drift away.

A heron swoops down on the bank opposite. We stay deadly still and see its head bend toward the damp grass, its beak prod sharply into the soil. There's only the sound of the water passing us by.

"I'll show you my favorite bit," Dean says.

We keep the river on our left, following where it's been. A bit further on, just before it curves, Dean stands still on the bank and starts to take off his shoes and socks.

"Coming?" he asks.

"Where?" I don't know how it's possible to have happy and sad so side by side. How my heart hurts more than it ever has, but I look at this boy and want to laugh into the blue.

"There." He points to a large rock sitting in the middle of the river. "It's not too deep to wade across." He rolls up the bottom of his jeans and steps into the clear water. "Just a bit cold."

I take off my shoes and socks as I watch him. The bottom of my jeans are damp from the long grass and hard to push up.

I step into the river and the water clamps my ankles in ice.

"Just a bit cold?" I laugh. "What's a lot cold, then?"

"Colder than this."

My feet burn and numb, before I reach the rock where he already sits, his legs stretched out in front of him. It's a small step onto it, but it juts high enough out of the water to keep us dry.

"This is your favorite bit, then?" I stretch my legs next to his, feeling my skin sparkle.

"Yup."

"It's a bit like the moon," I say.

"A very small moon."

"Maybe we're just very big." The gray stone is smooth under my palm. "If you're a giant, when we move on, it'll only take a few steps if you want to come and see me."

"I'll have to be careful not to squash your tent."

"It's too late. Everything's already been crushed."

Dean shields his eyes from the sun as he looks at me. "Does it feel that bad?"

"It's like my family is painted on a piece of material and Ma is ripping us right down the middle."

"Does anyone go on her side?"

"Rita might. But then I think she'll never forgive her. I don't know. I'm scared that everyone will hate my mom if I tell them what I saw," I say. "But then I'm scared that I'll have to carry this secret forever."

"I'm helping carry it."

"But tomorrow I'll be gone, and I won't see you."

Dean looks at me. "Do you really just move on and go? To the next place?"

"Yes."

"And that's it?"

"We leave our footprints." But my mind crashes and whirls because I don't just want to leave our footprints here. I want our wheels to stop for a while, for a little bit longer.

"How far do you go? After here?"

"Sometimes the next town, sometimes a bit further."

"So I could come and see you?"

"But a few days after that we'd move again. And again." The road will stretch too far between us. "It's impossible."

"Nothing's impossible," he says.

"Some things are."

Dean puts his hand into the water, just where it curls around the soft gray of the rock. It's only the tips of his fingers, but it's enough to make the river change direction, stumble confused a different way, before it carries on.

"That's a good color," Dean says, pointing to my painted toenails. "Proper bird-egg blue."

"Rita did them," I say, wiggling them to dry them more. The numbness in my ankles has almost gone. "I did hers luminous pink."

"Seems a shame to have them covered up by shoes most of the time."

"At least I know it's there," I say, pointing them straight. "You know, I bet there's loads of color around us that we can't see."

"What, underneath the bark of trees we'll find bright blue?"

"Maybe not bright, but there'll be blue." I look at Dean carefully. "Gramps told me that we only use some of our brain, the rest is a bit of a mystery. I reckon the world is like that too. There's tons we can't see. Like when you look into a sunbeam and suddenly there're millions of specks of dust floating right in front of your eyes, but you never normally know they're there." I turn to lie on my stomach. The sound of the river is stronger when I look at it. I dip my fingers in, hold them there in the cold.

"I reckon there are angels everywhere too, but we just can't see them," I say.

"Can't?" Dean says, turning onto his stomach too. "Or we don't know where to look?"

We lie so close together, there are only fragments of air between us. Dean puts his hands next to mine in the water.

"Let's leave palm prints," he says.

"Instead of footprints?"

"Yes. In the water."

I nod. "Rita would approve."

And so we press our hands into the river, and I tell it to remember us. To remember me and Dean together. The water takes the untold future in our palms and runs quickly away from us.

The sun dips suddenly behind the only cloud. It's instantly colder, but it won't be long before it appears the other side.

"I think my mom's a coward." The word tastes sour in my mouth. "If she was unhappy, she should've just said. If she wants to leave my dad, she should have the courage to tell us."

"Maybe she doesn't want to leave him? Maybe this is just a thing for her."

"A thing?" Rob and my mom. A thing. A thing that stamps on us and will rip us apart. "It's disgusting."

"I'm not saying she has a right to do it," Dean says hurriedly, as the sun strikes out again. "Just maybe it's not what you think it is. Maybe it was a one-off, a mistake."

It didn't look like that. I saw the way her skin was smiling as she put her shirt back on.

I sit up and wipe the river water on my jeans, smearing the material temporarily dark, before I shuffle forward on the rock and push my feet hard into the water. I need the cold to cut the image away.

"You'll be OK, Laura," Dean says.

"Will I?"

I look back over my shoulder at him. His eyes are half shut from the light as he watches me.

"Of course." I can't tell if he really means it. "Watch," he says. "Closely." His palms are flat down in the cold water. "Are you looking?"

"Yes," I tell him. He closes his fingers, the skin different under the surface. He opens them, turns them over and a stone sits in the middle of his right hand, snug among the lines of his fortune.

"Where did that come from?" I ask. He shrugs slightly, shyness creeping in on him. "It's clever," I tell him. "Will you do another?"

Dean takes his hands from the river and shakes them in the air. He moves to sit on the rock, his legs crossed over each other.

"Do you have a coin?" he asks. His eyes make my skin shine warm. "Any will do."

I reach into my pocket and pull out some loose coins. Dirty copper smell spills into the air.

"A two pence is fine," Dean says, so I hand one to him. "It's a normal coin, right?" he asks.

"Yes."

He holds it flat and covers it with his other hand, makes a small hole between his thumbs and blows into it, as though encouraging a fire. I don't take my eyes from his hands as he passes it back to me.

"Look," he says. But it seems exactly as I left it, no burnt edges or color dripping from it. Queenie's head smiling as it always does.

"What?" I ask as I turn it over. And she smiles at me from this side too. I turn it over, and her crown is there, her neck, her shoulders on both sides. "How did you do that?" I look up at him. Pride is wrapped in his smile. "That's amazing." I rub my thumb on the pictures on the coin, feel where the lines dip and rise to make it real. "Can you do other stuff?" I ask. "Bigger stuff?"

"Like what?"

"Like making our circus have a permanent home. Just for a few months, so I can see what it's like. And for longer if it's good."

"Would you stay here?" Dean asks.

"On this rock?" I laugh.

"Around here."

"Maybe." I feel my heart beat in time with my breathing, in time with my words. "I'd like to stand on a piece of earth and know it's mine, even if it's only for a bit. To be able to go away and come back to it."

"You'd really give it all up?"

"Sometimes I want to." Guilt licks at me. Guilt at betraying my mom and dad, at the thought that I'd let go of them.

"You'd leave your sister?"

Rita. "I'd keep her with me."

"What if she wouldn't come?"

I think of not hearing her voice every day. The way her laugh drags my own out. How sometimes we feel sewn together.

"I'd make her," I say. But they're heavy words and wrong and I know they don't work. I open my palm and look at the coin. And I have to let go of the patch of earth that my mind has already planted, watch the roots wither and twist brittle away.

RITA

I knock on Rob's door and barely have time to pull my hair over my shoulder before he opens it. I don't know how just seeing him now makes my heart stumble.

"Rita?"

"My Bridge class," I remind him.

"I hadn't forgotten," he says, but I can tell he has.

When he bought his van, before he joined our circus, he took out the passenger seat so he could have a proper front door. I step up now and follow him through the black curtain he's hung to separate his home from the cab. It's a different world back here, and it makes me want to curl up in it forever.

Rob's bed by the window has been changed into a sofa and I sit on it, leaning back against the cushions, pretending this is the most natural thing for me to do.

"Cup of tea? Coffee?" He's at the tiny cooker, reaching for his battered kettle under the sink's tap. "Or hot blackcurrant?"

"Tea please," I say, even though I don't like it.

"What are you making?" I ask, picking up some orange thread from the pile of colors in front of me. They're on the table he pulls up from the floor each day. When Lo and I first came in here and he showed us how it worked, we made him do it again and again. There was the floor and then there was a table and it seemed like magic to us.

"A dream-catcher," he says.

"It sounds like something Lil would like." I stop my childish laugh quick.

Rob sits next to me and the air secretly snatches my breath.

"You're meant to hang it by your bed and it makes your dreams good," he tells me. I look at him, but I don't know what to say. "No one wants bad dreams," he says.

There's a strange pause I want to fill with so many things that my mind can't think. Rob leans forward and picks up a crooked circle. "So that's where these come in. But it's more difficult than I thought. I've done the outside part, and now it's all these complicated moves with all of these." He takes the thread from my hand and holds it up. "Somehow, this is meant to end up like a beautiful spider's web."

"I could help," I say. The kettle whistles suddenly as steam falls from it. Rob gets up, and I watch as he takes two mugs from hooks on the wall, opens a tin, and takes out two tea bags.

"Milk? Sugar?" He turns to me.

"Just milk. Thanks."

I feel new, but somehow as if I've always been here. Rob takes a teaspoon from the drawer, stirs in the boiling water, takes milk from the fridge and pours its white into the mug to turn it caramel brown. He squeezes out the tea bags and throws them together into his bin under the sink.

"There you go," he says, passing a mug to me. "Careful, it's hot."

I try not to put it on the table too quick, even though the heat pinches my fingers.

"Are there instructions for your dream-catcher?" I ask, as Rob sits next to me again.

"I'm kind of winging it," he says. "I've got a picture of one, and I'm going from there." He pulls out a piece of paper from under the pile of threads.

"You've got to copy that?" It's beautiful, but it's a difficult pattern of twisted, connected lines.

"It can't be too hard."

"You'll definitely need help," I say.

"And you're the woman for the job?" Woman.

"I could be." I smile at him and wonder what else it is I'm saying and wonder if he even hears it.

"So, Ash not with you today?" he asks.

"We're not together all the time."

"Will there be the sound of wedding bells soon?" He nudges me gently.

"I don't think so." I try to laugh with him, but I feel like I'm betraying Ash.

"Why not?" Rob asks, more serious now.

"He's my best friend." I pick up the waiting dream-catcher from the table and turn its colored circle in my hands.

"That's a good start for a relationship."

I shrug as though I don't care, when I know how much I do.

"I don't always feel it."

"You think there should be more?"

I want to feel like Lo does with Dean. The way she lights up.

"I don't know."

Rob's so close to me that it makes my skin ache.

"Rob." Tricks's voice bursts through the front door. Rob jumps up, the top of his tea knocked from his mug as he bumps into the table. He goes through the black curtain, and I hear as he opens his door.

"The back flight of steps is playing up again," Tricks says.

"It's that same hinge, I think."

"No problem," Rob says. "Give me one minute. I'll meet you there."

"Thanks." And the door closes and Rob is here, hooking the curtain back with his hand. He doesn't come back in.

"Sorry, Rita, I've got to help Tricks out."

"That's OK." I look to my mug of tea still hot and untouched on the table. As I stand up, I wish I could take the feeling from this van with me. "But will you teach me Bridge another time?" I ask. Rob steps far back as I pass him.

"Of course," is all he says.

And I step down and out into the air.

Chapter Five

LO

Our big top waits for the evening performance. It's empty of strangers now, but the smell of them and their dreams stays locked under the canvas. Even leaving the door rolled open doesn't send it away.

I see the back of Spider, standing in the middle of the ring. He's holding the end of the wire, and high above him Tricks works on the clips that keep it safe. The seats all around look like rows and rows of gaping mouths.

Spider hears me as soon as I step over the threshold.

"You OK?" he asks quietly when I get to him.

"Not really."

"Do you want to talk?"

"No." I look up at Tricks, wound tight in the black clothes he rarely changes from. If it was a dark night above him, his body would disappear. He'd be a floating white face. A strange bob of a star.

"It feels like you've been avoiding me," Spider says.

"Well, I haven't been."

"Can we just forget what we saw?" he asks quietly. "Go back to how we were?"

"OK," I say, as he moves the wire slightly.

"You're being different."

"Am I?"

But I know I am. It feels like something is cutting through our friendship, but I can't tell whether it's Ma or my secret of Dean.

"Where've you been going?" Spider asks. "Sometimes I can't find you anywhere."

"Then you haven't been looking in the right places."

"Lo?"

Above us, Tricks is caught too tight in his work to hear me.

"I met Dean again," I say.

"That boy from the fountain?" Spider looks shocked.

"Yes. He's nice."

"Does anyone know?"

"Only Rita."

I shouldn't have told him. I can see his thoughts making no sense behind his eyes.

"Do you hate Rob?" I ask him.

"I thought you wanted to forget it," he says.

"I try, but I can't."

Everything is strange now. This town with its unlucky coins that took my mom away, but gave me a boy on broken glass and moon stones.

"Don't tell anyone, Spider. About any of it."

"I won't."

"You mustn't."

"Hold it straight," Tricks snaps down. Spider looks up and locks his arm to steady the wire.

"Do you hate my mom?" I whisper.

"No." But he doesn't turn his eyes to me.

"I don't want you to hate her," I say.

"I don't." His neck is tense. The secret we know floats between us. "I'm sad, though. I thought she was better than that."

Pinpricks of shame and anger fight to find a place in me.

"She's still my mom," I say.

"I know."

"Why did you have to look in Rob's van in any case?" I know I shouldn't say it. I know my anger is putting me too close to Spider's secret, which he doesn't want to share.

I turn and run away from him before I can say any more, and I leave him with the empty chairs who've heard it all but can't say a word. And Tricks, oblivious above his head, his hands and mind twisted in with the bolts at the end of the wire, our line between life and death.

Gramps sits in Mada with no light on, the curtains in the kitchen half closed.

"Lass," he says when I stumble inside.

I go over and sit on the floor by his feet, curl my legs under, and lean my head against his knees. His hand strokes my hair, as though no years have passed since he was younger and I didn't know that he'd really get old.

"What is it, Lo?" But I can't tell him. I can't ask him if he knows.

"Things are just wrong." He must know I am crying. My tears soak through his trousers to his bones, as he strokes my hair.

"When you were born," he says, "my Margaret said you were a fallen star to earth. She knew that there was something special about you. That you had shine inside your eyes." His words should make me happy, but they push my sadness deeper.

"Lo?" I hadn't heard Rita come in. Gramps stops speaking, and I know he must look up at her. "What's wrong?" She kneels down beside me, moves me away from Gramps's knees and brushes my tangled hair from my face. "What is it?"

I shake my head at her.

"Lo? Is it Ma? Dad? What's happened?"

"Nothing," I say, when I realize her panic. "They're fine."

"Why are you upset, then?"

"It's nothing."

Her eyes narrow at me. "Is it Dean? Have you seen him again? Has he hurt you?"

I know Gramps hears it all.

"No. He wouldn't."

She stands, hands on hips, waiting, but I've got no answer I can give her.

"I just felt sad, is all," I say.

"That's a lot of tears for no real reason."

"You've done it before," I say, feeling Gramps's fingers lift from my hair. I get up clumsily, heavier than before, when I should feel lighter after all the crying.

Rita leans over and hugs me so tight I think my bones will break.

"Ma asked me to get lunch sorted," she says, going over to the cupboards. "She says there's some chicken stew left from last night, and I'll do potatoes. Is that OK for you, Gramps?"

"That'll be perfect," he says, looking over to the place where our mom should be.

★ ★ ★

I think of Dean as Rita and I wait behind the ring door curtains. The wind knocks the sides of the tent, and deeper inside, our music sucks the air dry.

Rob and Tricks stand talking to the side of us. Tricks is the one with the painted face, but it should be Rob. My skin feels empty, standing so close to him. Everything I know and thought and loved has been ripped and scattered, and I don't know who he is any more.

Gramps pulls back the curtain, and Stanley and Spider come rushing through. They breathe heavily as they pass us, Stanley patting Spider on the shoulder, taking the swords from him.

I run to stand in the middle of the ring, surrounded by strangers who wait for something spectacular to weave into their stories. They don't see that my smile is stuck on over a mouth that wants to scream.

I open the middle of the giant plastic bubble hanging from the roof, climb in and close it behind me. I see Sarah—the stolen human child—do the same. I mirror her, moving my legs up the curve of the ball, as Dad and Rob pull the ropes to lift us higher. They work together, and still my dad doesn't know.

I balance angry in the air, turning slowly. We're two girls, with bodies twisted in bubbles that don't burst. The change-ling child and the one whose life has been stolen. Sarah opens her feathers as we crack our bodies in two, our muscles bending in the way they know. As simple as breathing.

And as we spin, I close my eyes and try to hold the world still. The people watching see me here, but in my head, I'm gone. I'm running to Dean, telling him to follow me. He reaches for me, but his mom pulls him back and he spins away.

I curl my wings around as the bubble slows and the ground comes closer, until it's here enough for me to open the plastic.

Sarah and I step out. We wave to the blur of hands and moving light sticks, as the audience calls for us, two beaming girls, their skin sewn with sequins. If only they could see inside.

When we walk off, Gramps closes the ring door curtains behind us. Rob's smile is wide, and he tries to hug me as he normally does, but I leave my hands by my side.

"Lo?" he asks. I just shrug and move away, letting him and Tricks through.

"What's up?" Rita asks, as Rob disappears into the ring.

"I'm not feeling well," is all I say to her and it's not a lie. My bones feel splintered.

*   *   *

I let Rita tell Ash about Dean. She wouldn't come to the skate park without him and Spider, especially not in the dark. I know he's not happy as he walks with us now, his face unsure as we keep close together.

"You're sure it's not some elaborate trap?" Spider asks.

"What, and they ambush us?" I say.

"It happens," Rita says.

"It's OK," I say, wanting to chase away her nerves. "Dean told me to come."

"But how much do you really know him?" Spider asks.

"I know him enough." I link my arm with his, steadying him through his doubt.

We turn the corner and see the skate park sitting strangely in the next stretch of grass. There are lots of people not like us, huddled and split and spinning down the concrete dips and hills.

"We could turn back," Rita says.

"You can, if you want," I say.

"Can you even see him?" Ash asks.

There are so many of them, faces getting clearer as we get closer. I look at each of the boys, but none of them are Dean.

Tall lights guard the area, and the dark fades as we near them.

"What shall we do?" Spider asks. He's nervous, and I'm not used to that.

"We'll look for him." I keep my head up high, my shoulders back, shaking my bracelets on my wrist gently just to hear their familiar noise.

At the line of the skate pit, where the grass ends and the concrete starts, a few people watch us. But they're not our audience here. It's different, and we're all on solid land together. I hold tight to Spider's arm and feel Rita and Ash get closer.

We stop to see the girl in front of us stand one foot on her skateboard and push hard away. She balances slouched but steady, as though she's not even thinking. She jumps the board up, and it scratches fast along a low metal pole before she skates off the other side.

There's a strange electric feel in the air that sits bright on my skin. "See. It's worth coming for this," I say. For a moment, I forget about Dean, about needing to see him, because there are so many people, boys and girls in jeans, with caps keeping their eyes hidden from the moon. There's the steady sound of wheels spinning on smooth concrete, the thud of boards.

"They're looking at us," Rita says to me, pulling on my sleeve, her eyes dipped in a fear I haven't seen before.

"It's OK," I tell her, because it is. "This is living, Rita."

It's Ash who puts his arm around her and pulls her close, and she lets him.

"We can go back," he says.

"I'm not leaving Lo," she replies, but she doesn't pull away from him as she sometimes does.

"I've got Spider," I tell her.

"I'm staying," Rita says.

And then I spot him. Even with his back toward us, I know it's Dean. The way he stands. Just the way he is.

"Come on," I say.

We walk quietly behind the uneven circle of people, behind those standing and talking and disappearing down into the concrete bowls. I try to pretend that no one watches us, that no eyes follow these strangers with circus blood.

"Hey," I say, and he turns before my hand even touches his shoulder.

"Laura," he says, his smile instant. He's standing with a boy I haven't seen before. Spider quickly unhooks his arm from mine and we're all awkward, out of place as Rita said we would be.

"I'm glad you came," Dean says, looking just at me.

"I said I would." I want to hold his hand but I know I can't.

A boy stands tall on pedals and lets his bicycle drop over the ridge. He speeds fast down and flies up high the other side, his front wheel twisting above the horizon line, before spinning down again.

It feels like there's a wire threading from him to us as we watch and it winds around everyone here. It's a different adrenaline to the one I know. One that I can taste. One that burns my toes and makes me want to try it all.

"Can you do stuff on that?" It's Spider who breaks the spell, nodding to the skateboard Dean has leaning against his knees.

"Kind of," Dean says and the boy beside him sneers.

"What?" I challenge. The boy looks surprised—that this strange girl speaks to him.

"He's good." The boy's eyes level with mine.

"Can we see?" Spider asks. Dean looks to me.

"We'd like to," I tell him and he smiles back at me in a way that sparks fire in my veins.

Dean flips down his skateboard, tips it and steps quickly on before the wheels run down the gray wall and up the other side.

In the air, his feet stick magnetic to his board as he holds the end of it, stopping time. He bends his knees and twists his body before he's facing down again, coming back toward us, stepping onto the level ground at our feet.

"I thought he said you were good," I laugh.

"You should join our circus," Spider says. I don't think I've ever seen him so impressed.

"It can't be that hard," Ash says. "You could ride one of those through fire, Spider."

The boy next to Dean looks toward us.

"The circus?" he asks and something in the atmosphere snaps.

"Yes," Spider says.

"You're pikeys?"

"They're cool, Ben," Dean says.

"Can we see more?" I ask, trying to smooth out the sudden jagged air.

"We should go," Ash says.

"Why?" the boy says. "Our tricks not good enough for you?"

"They're very good," Ash says. "We've just got to go."

"Back to your traveling fleapit?"

"Ben," Dean says.

"What? You must've heard of dancing fleas?"

"Give it a rest," Dean says.

"You're not friends with them, are you?" Ben's eyes spark ridiculous, his eyebrows arched into perfect thick lines.

I look at Dean, but he doesn't hesitate.

"Yes," he says. "They're all right."

"Why wouldn't we be?" Ash asks.

"Let's go." Rita starts to pull Ash away.

"You're not all right," Ben says. "Because you're pikey scum." Spider moves straight toward him, stands taller, so close their chests are almost touching.

"Don't call us that again," Spider says. The wheels of skateboards have stopped. Boys sit watching on their bikes. It feels like they're stepping closer, but they stay where they are.

"I say what I see, circus scuzz-boy."

Spider pushes him hard in the chest, enough to make Ben lose balance and have to run awkward down the slope. Humiliation follows his every step.

"We're going." Ash pulls on Spider's arm.

"Do you have to?" Dean looks at me. But Ben is walking too fast up the bowl toward us.

"Yes."

We turn, but I won't run. I won't let Ben know that he's won. That our strangeness couldn't give us even one evening with them.

We're on the edge of where the floodlight changes into darkness when Spider suddenly spins and falls. Ben is standing next to us, breathing heavy. Spider huddles, stunned. He's bleeding. This boy made Spider bleed.

"You hit him." My words sit in the blurred bright air.

Ash is pulling Spider up. Blood drips in streaks from his nose.

"Tip your head back," Ash tells him, wiping at Spider's blood with his sleeve.

"Why did you do it?" I shout at Ben, but he just forces a laugh and turns away from us.

"Are you going to leave it?" I ask Ash, anger burning my breath tight.

"Yes," Spider says.

"You need to go, Laura." It's Dean, his voice soft in this madness.

"You're going to let him get away with it?"

"He's a nut job. It's his way of communicating."

"Thumping people?"

"He's not a friend of mine," Dean says quickly. "I only know him from down here."

"Lo, we're going," Rita says. She's pulling on my arm and I let her. I don't want to be here anymore.

"You can keep your world," I say to Dean, as we walk away. "You can keep this life." But a pain breaks open in my chest as I say it.

"Laura." His voice travels toward me.

But I don't look back. Spider's blood still spills from his nose and it's enough to make me follow the line that pulls us home.

RITA

"We're different, us and them," I tell Lo. I'm glad we're leaving tomorrow so she never has to see Dean again.

"Don't be stupid, Rita," she says, her voice a bit adrift.

"I'm not."

"How many eyes have you got?" Lo asks, sitting on her bed.

"Two," I say.

"Heart?"

"One."

"Belly?"

"One."

"So have they," Lo says. "They're not different at all."

"You know what I'm saying."

"I don't. Because you're wrong. It doesn't take a genius to work out that deep down we're all the same." She rolls her sock all the way down her ankle and off her foot.

"Don't you mind that Spider was hurt?"

"You know I do." Lo is about to throw her sock into our laundry basket, tucked in the corner, but she stops and looks up at me, confusion strong in her eyes. "But it wasn't Dean's fault."

"He mixes with them."

"Maybe he's not got much choice." She gets up, puts her sock in the basket, and pulls the other off to join it. "It's a small town," she says, sitting back heavily on her bed. "There aren't many people to choose from."

"It doesn't mean he has to be friends with them."

"Since when did you turn into Dad?" Lo asks me, slipping under her duvet and pulling it tight up to her chin. Only her head sticks out, her blonde hair spikey but smooth all at once.

"I'm scared you're going to get hurt," I tell her and the bubbling anger in her eyes switches quickly softer.

"I'll be fine," she says. "You should be more worried about Miss Ladder Witch. I hear she's waiting with sharpened claws tonight." And she makes her eyes go cross-eyed.

"Thanks for that," I say.

"You're welcome," she laughs and she watches as I put my hands on the wood against my mattress, step onto her bed and haul myself up to my own, banging my knee and the edge of my foot.

"Safely there?" Lo asks.

I leave a silence, but I know she won't be worried.

"Maybe," I say and she gives me her laugh as a reply.

* * *

"Just in time for pancakes," Dad says. A stack of them sits in the middle of the table in front of him. I can hear Ma vacuuming their bedroom. When Lo comes in their front door, Dad doesn't seem to notice the strange feeling that follows her.

"Morning, Gramps," Lo says, and she goes to kiss him, but I know her mind is miles away, too twisted up with thoughts of Dean and flatties who hit and worlds we'll never know or understand.

"Blueberry or maple syrup?" Dad asks.

"I'm not really hungry, Dad," Lo says. "I'm going to see Spider."

"You'll eat your breakfast first. Ma has spent time preparing it." There's a certainty in his voice that she won't work around. A crackling of anger she won't want to fuse. And so she takes a plate from him, slapping it heavy on the tablecloth as she sits down.

I scrape the knife across the butter and spread it melting onto my pancake before I pour a puddle of syrup that spills from it onto the plate. Lo rolls hers up without any filling and eats it plain.

"They're getting cold, Liz," Dad shouts when the noise of the vacuum stops. Their bedroom door opens and Ma comes in. She's wearing her red shirt, the one with patterns down the front, and she looks beautiful.

"Morning," she says, ruffling Lo's hair. If she realizes there's an unsteady mood around Lo, she doesn't say. "Anyone want chocolate sprinkles?" she asks, getting them from the cupboard before anyone replies. She sits next to me and puts a pancake on her plate. "So moving on today."

"I'm looking forward to the sea," I say.

"It's the pitch we were on two years ago," Dad says. "Right next to the beach."

"Got your bucket and spade, Gramps?" I ask. "Ready for the pier?"

"Bring on the bright lights." Gramps's laugh swoops around to pick us all up.

"Do you remember the storm last time, Liz?" Dad asks.

"Almost carried the big top out to sea."

"And Lo insisted on going on that donkey." Ma's back is straight as she eats.

"But you tried to stand on it," I remind Lo. "And it bucked you off," I laugh.

"It wasn't funny," Lo says.

Dad puts another pancake on her plate. "You need to eat one more before you go out," he says.

"Is it the same place where some flatties stole some of Helen's jewelry?" I ask.

"That'd be about right," Dad says, squeezing lemon to drip sour on his plate.

"They're not all bad," Lo says.

"Of course not," Ma says.

"Why are you so frightened of them, Dad?" Lo asks. I try to catch her eye, to warn her that she's stepping too close to a line.

"Frightened of them? Enough of your cheek," Dad says. "We just need to keep the circus blood going, or there'll be no circus." He pours a covering of sprinkles on what's left of his pancake.

"He just wouldn't want to lose any of you to a flattie," Ma says.

"We've lost enough, Liz." Dad is serious now. "Any more and soon it'll be just you and me, and no one's going to pay to see that."

"Lo and I would," I say, but she's quiet now, eating her last mouthful, getting up quickly, and stomping heavy to the sink.

I finish my breakfast as Lo crashes through the washing-up, putting silverware in the drawer barely dry. I don't say anything, though, and together we leave Mada before anyone asks her why.

It's a sunny day outside, but Lo doesn't even notice. Normally she'd be the first to call out to the blue sky, yet now her thoughts are crammed too tight with Dean. Maybe I'm pleased that we're moving on today and there'll be a new town and she'll be able to forget him and be happy again.

With Spider's van empty, we know to find him at his parents'. When we knock, it's Helen who opens their door. I've never seen her scowl, but her face has fallen into the crease of one now.

"He told me he fell over," is all she says, the crinkled hiss of fatty bacon following her words.

"Is he OK?" I ask.

"I know the look of a thumped nose," she says. "Have you got him into trouble?" She stares hard at Lo.

"Why's it got to do with me?" Lo asks. This is a strange place to be. Helen is like a second mom to us all.

"Well it wouldn't be Rita here, would it?"

"Can we see him?" Lo asks.

"Be my guest." Helen sweeps up her anger and steps back. Inside, Spider and his dad sit in silence at the table. The skin around Spider's eye is bubbled green and his nose is swollen red.

"Does it hurt?" Lo asks quietly as she breathes in.

"I'm fine," Spider says.

"He's not," Helen interrupts, pushing past us with two plates heavy with breakfast.

"It's just a knock," his dad says. He picks up his knife and fork and doesn't even wait for Helen to join them before he cuts dead through the cooked yellow of his egg.

"God only knows what Tricks is going to say," Helen says, putting down her own plate and laying her napkin flat across her knees.

"With moving on and set-up, it'll be a couple of days before he's in front of the public," Ernest says. "And by then any bruise that's left can be covered with greasepaint." He picks up his triangle of toast and swipes it through the fat leaked onto his plate.

"I think we'd like to eat breakfast in peace," Helen says.

"Mom." Spider almost winces with embarrassment. Since we were children, his parents' van has been like home to us.

"It's OK," Lo says. I think she's as desperate as I am to get away. "We'll see you when you've finished, Spider."

He nods at us, unsmiling, his knife cutting back and forth through the thick bacon, and we leave them, Lo closing their door soft behind us.

"Don't say it," she says as we walk across the grass.

"Say what?"

"That it's my fault Spider got hurt."

"I wasn't going to. I was going to say that Spider will be OK." Lo's biting her nail in a way she hasn't done since she was a little girl, ripping at the skin, deep enough to make it almost bleed.

"You really like Dean, don't you?" I ask quietly, following her under the heavy curtain of the big top, but she doesn't answer.

Someone has already been in here this morning as the lights are on. They're not warm enough to feel them on our skin, though.

Lo goes and stands at the edge of the seats, her arms hanging loose by her sides, her head tipped looking up as though catching raindrops.

"Is this all there is, Rita?" she asks quietly. Her words so unexpected make me want to cry.

"Aren't you happy?" I ask.

"I am," she answers. "But is it enough?"

"Enough of what?"

She looks down and starts to sweep her foot in a circle on the ground.

"I knew you wouldn't understand," she says.

"But I don't know what I'm meant to understand."

Lo looks at me. "Don't you ever want to change? Be someone else for a bit?"

"We're someone else every night. Every night that we perform."

"But for longer. Change completely. Maybe just for a bit, but live a different life."

"A different life to the circus?"

"Yes." She looks so guilty, so lost, and it makes me want to wrap her up in all we've got so that she can see.

"Why would you want something different to the circus? How can you forget how magical it is?"

"I haven't," she says. "I never will."

"Rob grew up outside the circus and he says he felt stuck. It was like being claustrophobic all the time. There was no freedom, Lo."

"So now he thinks he's free to just do what he wants?" she snaps back.

"Of course. We all are."

"Even if it destroys others?"

"What do you mean?" She's switched so quick to anger and I don't know why. "You're talking nonsense, Lo."

"Am I?" I think she might laugh, or cry, or both.

"Is this because of Dean?" I ask, my annoyance creeping up to match hers. "He's been putting strange stuff in your head?"

"No."

"It is. You were fine until you met him."

She's never looked at me in this way, and it strips layers from my lungs in an instant.

"You don't know anything, Rita," she says, before she runs away, across the empty ring. As she lifts back the curtain, I see

Tricks standing there. He watches her rush past him before he steps through.

"What's up with Lo?" he asks.

"Nothing," I say. But how much has he heard? Did her words reach him?

"It didn't look like nothing."

"It was, really, Tricks. It's just Lo being Lo." And I go from him quickly, even though he's concerned.

As I step outside, a hand reaches out to hold mine. It's Ash.

"Are you OK, Rita?" he asks. But he seems so young to me all of a sudden, that his kindness is useless and he won't know how to help.

"I'm fine," I say. Because I can't tell anyone that Lo's mind is tumbling.

"Do you want to go for a walk?"

"No," I say. I don't mean it to sound harsh, and I know I've upset him. "I just don't want to, is all."

"You could come to mine, if you want?"

"Why can't you leave me alone, Ash?" I'm shocked by my sharpness, but the sadness on his face makes me angry. I'm fed up of the games, his little-boy eyes. "I wish you'd just grow up a bit." And before I can regret saying it, I turn from him and run away.

Chapter Six

LO

I'm folding the tent's ropes when I see him, standing on the edge of the park. By the wall where I sat with Spider when my world began to change.

The striped canvas has been hauled down and sits loose on the grass. Rita once said our big top looks like a giant dying jellyfish when it's like this, and now that's what I see as it settles slowly to the ground. I'm meant to help roll it up in the exact way it has to be, but instead I walk away.

I know they might see, but I have to go to him.

"Lo," Tricks calls to me.

"I'll be a minute," I say, waving him away.

As I walk across the grass, Ma and Rob's bare skin lifts away from me and I see only Dean. He half waves when he sees me, but he hesitates. Maybe he's unsure about coming closer to our homes, maybe unsure whether I'll want to speak to him after last night.

I meet him by the wall. "The pikeys won't bite," I say,

nodding to my family far behind me.

He looks like I've slapped him. "Ben's nothing to do with me."

"You didn't exactly do much to stand up for us."

"I did. After you'd left." He reaches out to try to hold my hand, but I pull my arm away. "If I'd said something when you were there, it would've made things worse." I look away from him, concentrating on a tree breaking through the pavement, its leaves hanging high over the road. "Honestly, Laura. What you saw yesterday was nothing. Ben kicks off all the time, on anyone."

"And no one does anything?"

"Not everything about my world is good."

I look up at him, and I want him to know that I'm sorry for my spikey words. I know he hears me. No one has ever looked to my very bones.

"I was hoping we'd go to the river again," he says.

"I haven't got time," I say, my barriers completely gone. "After pack-up we're moving on."

"I want to come and see you, Laura."

"How will you, though?"

"I'll drive, it's not far. I'm insured on my mom's car."

"You'd really come?"

"Of course," he says.

I want to kiss him, and I wonder if he would kiss me back, if we weren't here where people might see. Instead we stand, our fingers touching.

Dean looks at me. "How will I know where you are when I get there?"

"We're pitched right next to the sea. You won't be able to miss us."

"And I just come in?"

"I'll look out for you," I say.

"Which is your van?"

"Terini," I say. "It's written above the door." And Dean nods.

"But be careful."

"Lo?" The shout echoes out toward us.

"Tricks isn't happy," I say. "He likes us all to pull our weight."

"I promise I'll find you," Dean says.

And he bends his head down slightly and kisses me quickly on the lips.

I want to take this moment, trap it tight in a bottle.

"Lo!" I hear Tricks shout again.

"I have to go."

I move my hand from his, and I have to walk away from him. From the boy who makes my blood spark in a way I've never known.

I look back and he's still standing there, his hands in his pockets.

I wave, but it doesn't feel enough. Nothing does, as I turn from him again and walk back to the mess my family has become.

The inside of the car makes my head ache. It feels like the doors have trapped me inside, moving me on when I'm not ready yet. Taking me to an unsteady place, when I want to stay with Dean.

Everyone else is happy. My dad is even humming to himself when we first spot the sea.

"There it is," he says, as though no one else has seen it. Rita reaches over the gap between us and squeezes my hand.

Dad glances at us in the rear-view mirror.

"Everything all right, Lo?" he asks.

I can't tell him anything, about Ma, about my moon-rock boy and the secrets I've given him.

"She's just a bit worried about Gramps, is all," Rita says.

"Gramps?" Dad asks.

"That he's getting older."

I can tell that Dad is surprised, that he wasn't expecting it.

"Better to be getting older than younger," he says, trying to take the thoughts away.

"I don't know," Ma says. "Getting younger would be OK." She's there, with Rob, her skin young enough for him. I have to close my teeth together to stop myself from screaming.

"Will it be warm enough to swim?" Rita asks.

"Only if you want to freeze to death," Dad says.

"I can hear seagulls," Ma says. She leans forward to look up through the front window. Above, I see just one bird floating, its white wings wide. We're close enough to see the tips of its beak slightly parted. If I could turn small, I'd clutch onto its back and tell it to fly me to Dean.

Our car turns onto the grass, following the one in front with its van attached. I can see the edge of Tricks's car, where Gramps likes to travel. I know he'll have the tin of sugared sweets on his lap and he'll be making shapes with the crinkled wrappers in his hands.

I can smell the sea as soon as I get out. And I can hear it. Dad walks around and puts his arm over Ma's shoulder. She doesn't pull away.

"It's good here, isn't it?" he says.

I don't want to see the lie in her face. Instead, I turn to Rita, needing to do the handshake that we always do when we arrive at a new place. But she's already walking off to where Ernest has parked Terini.

RITA

Magic happens when we set up our site. Before, there's just a blank stretch of grass and then slowly everything we need seems to grow out of the ground. When we used to be too tiny to help, Lo and I would sit and watch as the frame of the big top was winched up. It was our robot, so tall its head was almost in the clouds, webs of metal waiting for clothes. The stacks of chairs a thousand teeth waiting to eat the flatties whole.

It's windy today and the tent is struggling against us. I thought it'd like it here, with its view of the sea.

"I think it wants to swim," I tell Ash, as we help haul it and hold it in place.

"The tent?" And he laughs at me, shaking his head. Rob appears and instantly the air feels electric.

"We could sail on it to Norway," Ash says. He doesn't feel the change, and I wish I could stop myself noticing too.

"Wanting a holiday?" Rob has a deeper laugh than Ash, and it creeps happy under my skin.

"Never," I say. Ash finishes looping the rope and stands straight.

He's almost as tall as Rob, but next to him he somehow looks like a boy again. "Are you going to come and watch Carla on the pier?"

"Her silver woman statue?" Rob says.

"She's good at it," Ash says, defensive of his mom. "Sarah is going to do it too."

"I can't come," Rob says. He touches my arm so quick that

I wonder if Ash even sees. I feel it, though. "You all go and tell me what you think when you come back."

"We will," I say.

"Enjoy," Rob says and I try not to let his smile touch me, not in front of Ash.

We watch him as he walks away.

"I've seen my mom practicing the statue. It's really good," Ash says, as Rob disappears around the side of the tent and I try to pretend that I don't feel empty.

"She'll be great, Ash," I say. But I don't want to be here. I want to have followed Rob and still be by his side.

"You OK?" Ash asks.

"Of course," I reply. He doesn't seem to notice my stage smile. I don't want him to ask more, so I turn from him and run across the grass and up Spider's van steps and already I'm banging on his door.

The wind catches underneath the clouds as we walk along the pavement by the sea. Lo's strange mood has left her, and she jumps onto Spider's back and he runs with her, darting among the flatties walking by. They don't seem to notice the blackening bruise on his cheek, uncovered by greasepaint.

Ash reaches for my hand, where it's usually comfortable, but instead I take the band from my hair and spend time doing and undoing my ponytail.

The pier stands steady in the water, busy with lights and noise that creep up on us as we get closer.

"What's up, Rita?" Ash asks. His question rocks the air slightly, and I don't like it. It leads me toward thoughts that rub awkwardly against each other.

"Everything's fine, Ash." And I link my arm through his. "The beach is beautiful, isn't it?" The sand reaches so wide to the sea, with only a few people walking on it, wrapped thick with clothes.

"What are they doing?" I laugh, watching as Spider stumbles from the steps onto the sand. He doesn't fall—he never would when he's holding Lo. Instead he walks like a drunken man, zigzagging across the beach.

We follow them, enough in time to see Lo jump down and throw herself back into the sand, her arms and legs moving in arcs around her.

"A sand angel," she laughs as we get to her. Spider lies down next to her, copies her every move. Sand splashes up into his face and paints his bruise speckled, as he spits the grains from his mouth, blinking it out of his eyes. Lo puts her hand out for me, and I pull her up.

"It needs a bit of work," I say. Ash runs down to the shore, not close enough for the sea to grab him, and he comes back with a trail of seaweed.

"For your angel, my lady," he says to Lo, laying it across her sand figure's head.

"Don't I get a crown?" Spider asks as Lo pulls him up. She holds her head down and shakes the cold grains from her hair.

"You get this." Ash picks up a broken plastic cup and balances it carefully on the sand where Spider's head was.

"Nice. Thanks," Spider says, wiping his hands against each other. He bends down and picks up the cracked cup, filling its good half with sand. "For you," he says, throwing it. Ash runs just in time, so Spider scoops up more. He's not as tall as Ash, but he's quick.

"Your lovely laugh," I tell Lo, looping my arm through hers. I don't want to tell her how much I've missed it, how the walls of our room have felt stripped and empty the last few days.

"Let's leave our footprints," she says.

And we hold each other as we stand together, one foot each pressed side by side into the sand.

There are still people on the pier, even though the summer is behind us and here the wind from the sea feels even stronger on our skin.

"There they are." Lo points to where Carla and Sarah sit twisted together on a mat, their silver feet arched over their backs, nestled next to their silver hands.

"They look freaky even to me," Ash says. People gather around them, but not too close. A woman bends down to a child and together they throw a coin into the hat by Carla's mat. Slowly, she untangles herself, points her legs straight in the air and balances on one arm, her other stretched out to the side. And she stops and doesn't move as she and Sarah wait.

"That's gonna hurt," Spider says, glancing around and waiting for someone to throw more coins in. The muscles in Carla's arms shake under the silver paint.

"She's got herself in a right mess now," Ash says. "She can't hold that forever."

Lo steps forward and throws in a coin. Carla's eyes switch quickly to her and away, the briefest tip of a smile on her lips. She turns her body crooked like a knotted branch, comfortable now without muscles burning, waiting for more cash to fall onto the mat.

LO

The flames in the barrel burn slowly. I sit with Rita close by my side, our backs to the murmuring traffic. If I threw a stone from here, it would almost land in the sea. It would have to fly over the thin promenade and the stretch of beach, but it might make it.

"I did," Rob says. "I once swam on Christmas Day."

"You never," Tricks says, the fire flickering yellow and dark on his cheek.

"When I was twenty-one."

Every word Rob says tacks onto me. I want to love him again, but his voice grinds sharp under my skin. It's the lies dripping from it. The fact that I don't even know who he is any more.

"Do you remember the last time we were here, Lo," Spider says. "You swam out to sea holding a cotton candy."

"I remember it," I say.

"Your toes and knees bobbed above the water," he laughs. "The pink fluff was bigger than your head."

"We used the stick for a flag for our sandcastle," Rita says.

"My sandcastle, I think you'll find," Ash says. "But I never got the credit for it."

He leans forward with his arms on his knees, his fingers linked into each other. Spider pokes him in the ribs, but Ash is too quick and topples him backward off the log.

"It's a beautiful night," Spider says, lying on his back, his legs sticking up to the sky.

"Who was the boy, then?" Tricks asks me.

"What boy?" I ask, but in the firelight my heart begins to beat quicker. He knows.

117

"The one you were with."

"Lo's not allowed a friend?" Rita asks.

Spider pulls himself back up, using Ash's arm to steady himself.

"Who is he?" Tricks asks.

"Dean," I say, trying to keep my voice steady. Trying to show them he's someone I can be proud of.

"Where did you meet him?" Rob asks. I don't see why he needs to know, but I know I have to stay calm.

"At a fountain," I say. It feels like my secret is drifting out of my reach.

"Does your dad know?" Tricks asks.

"There's nothing to know," Rita answers for me. "It's past tense. He's from the last town."

"Your dad will kill you if you keep seeing him." Ash is quieter this time.

"Ah, young love," Rob says. I think he might be trying to help me, but I hate him for it. I should be grateful, but instead I take the image of him with my mom and push it down into the flames.

"Who's in love?" It's Dad. I hadn't heard him on the grass.

"No one," Rita says.

Dad sits down next to Rob.

"You got yourself a girl, Rob?" Dad asks.

Rob laughs awkwardly. "Chance would be a fine thing."

I can barely breathe because my dad can't see the knife his friend is slicing clean through his heart. I know I can't stay sitting here, not when anger burns in me so hot that I'm scared about what I'll say.

"I'm going to bed."

"Already?" Spider asks me.

"You coming, Rita?" I reach out for her hand and she gets up.

"I suppose so."

"You don't have to." Ash looks disappointed.

"It's fine. I want to," she says.

"Night, Dad," I say, as I lean down to hug him close. "I love you." I scramble over the log, without saying anything to anyone else.

"Night all," I hear Rita say.

"See you in the morning." Rob is the only one to reply.

The dark air wraps cold around us as we head away from the fire. My thoughts are skittering, but at least I know that Ma is not with Rob right now. Maybe Dean is right, that it was just once, a strange mistake.

Back in Terini, Rita and I are quick to change and get into bed. The colder evenings bite our skin if we take too long.

"Lo?" Rita's voice filters down in the darkness.

"Mm."

"I need to tell you something, but you've got to promise me you won't tell anyone else."

"OK." My mind darts to Rob and Ma again. Does Rita know? Do we already share the secret?

"Say you promise," she says, the serious in her voice settling with my heartbeat.

"I promise."

"I think I love someone as well as Ash."

I didn't expect these words. "Who?" My mind flits to Spider. And Dean. But she can't love Dean.

"Rob."

"Rob?" Twists of cold touch my skin.

"Yes."

"Don't be stupid, Rita."

"I'm not. I think he likes me too."

"Stop joking. I'm not in the mood."

"I'm serious, Lo. And I don't know what to do about Ash. About any of it."

The air now buzzes thick between us. Too many thoughts block the blackness.

"I'm not listening anymore," I say, pulling my duvet tight around me, over my head so I can't hear.

But doubts and fear still creep in. My Rita and Rob? My sister with him? I slam the duvet away from me.

"Why do you think he likes you too?" I ask. "Have you done anything?" But I don't want to hear the answer. I don't want to know any of it.

"No," she says and relief pounds through me.

"It's just a stupid crush, Rita. With a stupid flattie who's waltzed in here with his big ideas, making out he's some special guy who wants to save us."

"But you love Rob too." Her voice is tiny.

"He's pathetic. I wish he'd never found us."

"You don't mean that."

"I do. And I also know that he doesn't love you, and he never will. It's all in your mind, Rita."

There's a silence and now I know she's crying, but Rob's name hangs like a wall between us, and I don't go to her.

"I just needed to talk to someone about it," she says.

I stand up and run out of the room, unlock our front door and stand unsteady on the steps. They're cold on my feet. Above me, the sky is a sparkling black.

Maybe this is what it's really like to fall from the edge of the world. Maybe I want to. Rob's unpicked the stitches of my life so I've nothing to stop me from letting go and tumbling off. I could untangle my thoughts up there, fall into the dark sky and never come back.

But I imagine Rita holding out her hand. My sister who'd walk tightropes of fire for me and would never let me go. So I reach up to pluck a star for luck, snatch it in my palm, before I open the door and go back inside. I step one foot on the bed's ladder, risking the witch's nails, and pull myself up beside her. She doesn't try to hide her tears.

"I don't know what to do," she says, her words breaking.

"It'll be OK," I say, stroking her hair. I can feel where her tears cling to it.

"It won't be." She's crying harder now, gulping for air as she tries to keep quiet.

"You just need to forget about Rob. Concentrate on Ash, Rita. He's kind and honest and he loves you."

But she doesn't answer.

★ ★ ★

I wake in the morning curled into Rita, as we always used to. Like cats, Ma would say. But today I'm cramped by the small space. My shoulders hurt and my elbows ache. I think Rita is asleep, but suddenly she clicks on her lamp, scrambles over me, and jumps from the bed.

She looks tired, but her tears have completely dried.

She's searching hurriedly through her clothes stacked neat in our cupboard.

"Rita?" I sit up, my head skimming the ceiling of our room.

"Mm," is all she replies.

"Are you OK?" I ask.

"It's a normal day, Lo," she says, as though the thought of her and Rob was never with us last night.

Our room suddenly feels too small, and I'm quick to dress.

* * *

The hood pulled over my head has turned the world musty brown. My breath pulls the material in close to my lips and pushes it out hot. Ma ties my arms spread wide and clips my ankles in so I can't move. She's the mother of the human child and thinks that if she pushes me close to death, the fairy queen will save me and swap me for her daughter.

The excitement steeps up around us. Dad will be show-ing the audience the knives, dramatically cutting material into shreds, pretending to lick the sharp blades.

Dean didn't come. My boy on the roof, who promised he would.

Above the music, I can hear the people clapping, hands slapping together like seals.

There's a thud by my ear, as Dad's first knife lands in the board that I'm tied to.

Dean held my hands and said he would come.

A thud close to my arm makes my fingers impulsively twitch, but I can't move.

Sitting on our moon rock, I felt safe to give him my thoughts. And he'd given me his.

A split second of wind against my cheek and the thud of the knife.

The music builds. The fairy queen hasn't come, so now Ma pushes the board around with me on it and I begin to feel everything spin.

The knife cracks next to my elbow, the next quickly by my ankle as planned.

Maybe I'll never see Dean again? The thought grabs at me too strong, as the final knife embeds above my head. They don't know that Dad could throw knives at me in his sleep and he'd always miss.

My mom will be slowing the spinning. The ground becomes still. My arms and legs are loosed enough for me to get free. Hands untie my blindfold and I stick on my wide smile, waving to the faces that merge into a blanket of cheering.

Ma tries to grab me, but I float under her arms and spin cartwheels to escape.

Rita peels the costume from her arms, turning her human again.

"A full house," Ma says, as she shakes her hair free from the beaded band that's kept it tight. "Rob will be pleased." Her reflection in the mirror shows that she doesn't know what her words have done to Rita, to me.

I rip off my feathers, stuff them roughly in the box. I want to tear my costume from me and then cut it into useless pieces. As soon as I'm in my clothes, I run away from them both, through the back door of our big top and away to the sea.

The wall to the promenade is low enough to step over. A boy on his tricycle stares at me, and I know I must look strange, my tears smearing my make-up thick down my cheeks.

I sit down in the sand, hugging my legs into me, watching the water rocking as I try to steady my world. Lay everything flat. I sit my mom and dad together, and they hold hands. Next to them, Rita sits with Ash. And at the end, balancing them all, is Dean. Just seeing him in my mind calms me.

Seaweed bubbles at the edge of the waves, as I breathe the salt air deep inside.

"Are you all right, Lo?" The voice is somewhere behind me. It's Gramps, walking slowly across the sand. "Admiring the sea?" He sits down, his brown coat crunching up around him. His yellow socks poke out the top of his shoes.

"It's beautiful," I say.

"It is." In front of us, the water stretches to the white sky.

"It's days like this that I miss Margaret more than ever." His breath wheezes slightly.

Margaret, my grandma. At two, I was too young to remember even her shadow. I only know her face from the photographs clustered on his bedroom walls. She looks warm and kind, with necklaces dripping from her and flowers nestled in her hair.

"The most beautiful girl you ever saw. She'd knock sequins off the rest of you," he chuckles. He forgets that he's told me this a million times before.

"It's a long time to miss someone," I say.

"Fourteen years." He nods.

"Is it very hard?"

He looks at me. It's a question I've never thought to ask before.

"It gets easier," he says.

I think of Dean, standing on the roof looking over the streets, and I ache inside. I barely know him, but missing him hurts enough.

"And I'd prefer to have loved her," Gramps says. "Even if it meant losing her." I hadn't realized that the stillness always sitting near him was Gramps missing his wife, his sparkling circus girl.

I can't tell whether I feel guilt or regret that I haven't shared his memories more, that we've left him too often in silence.

"Do you get lonely, Gramps?"

"Not anymore," he says. "At first, though, I couldn't see how I'd survive. Margaret was everywhere but nowhere. She was just there, but she was gone. Her make-up was in the bathroom, and I'd stare at the lipstick for hours because it was only half finished. It didn't make sense that she'd never put it on again. That it wouldn't be used."

I'd been so young. I hadn't noticed the grief that must have been sitting on his every word as I was growing up.

"I'm sorry," I say.

"None of it's your fault," he says warmly.

"But you were sad and I didn't know."

"Everyone gets sad, Lo. It's all part of living."

A seagull floats down, landing quietly just a few meters from us. It pecks and rips at a paper napkin caught in a bundle of seaweed.

"What's troubling you, then?" he asks. "Being out here on your own."

I dig my hand deep into the sand. It's cold underneath the surface and when I lift my fingers, the grains drip through and back onto the beach.

"Everything's gone wrong," I say. Ma and Rob. Rita loving blindly. Dean. I can't risk saying any more.

"Not everything, surely," he says. He nudges me gently with his shoulder. "The sun still rises every day, Lo. Things have a way of working out right in the end."

"But what about Grandma Margaret?"

"She wasn't scared of dying." His sigh is from deep inside him, from thoughts I'll never know. I make my eyes follow the perfect line of the horizon and imagine my grandmother watching us from the other side. "But when you lose someone, something happens. They leave you a gift. For the first time, you realize how precious life really is. And you learn to live properly, every day. You hear more and notice more. And you love more." I wait for him to say something else, but he's silent now. I wonder if he's walking hand in hand with his Margaret in his mind, and I don't want to disturb them.

Together we sit as the sea folds itself onto the beach, again and again. It wets the sand, dragging bubbles back with it. And all the time the sun sits on top of it. Gramps's sun that rises every day.

Chapter Seven

LO

I'm woken by a soft knocking on the door. It jumped into my dream, and it's made me instantly afraid.

"Rita?" I whisper, but there's no sound from her and the knocking is still here.

I get out of bed, crouch down, and look through a tiny crack in the curtain, but there's no one there.

"Lo?" I hear the whisper and I know it's him. I go to the door and open it and Dean stands on our steps, his coat wrapping him tight from the night-time cold. "Hey," he says.

"You came."

"I said I would." His eyes make my heart beat as he smiles.

"What time is it?" I ask.

"Four thirty."

"Four thirty!"

"I got up the same time as my mom. I thought we could go to the skate park."

"Now?" I whisper and the dark air scatters my laugh. "It's not even morning."

"I want to teach you." He holds up his board, the wheels still.

"There's a place just along from here. But maybe get dressed first?" He nods to the T-shirt that barely covers me. I've never been so naked in front of a boy. I'm normally covered with colors and thick tights invisible on my legs.

"I won't be long," I say.

I leave the door open slightly and sneak quietly into my room, pulling on my jeans, opening drawers softly so Rita doesn't wake. I can just see her shape lying sleeping in the dark, before I leave her.

Dean is standing on the grass now, darkness moving around him.

"I'm ready," I say, and he reaches to hold my hand.

Our site is silent and empty but for our circle of vans, and we cross it quickly.

"What's it like here?" he asks quietly.

"It's nice by the sea."

A car drives past and then the road is empty again.

"How are things?" he asks.

"Not great."

"Has your dad found out about your mom?"

"I don't know. I don't think so."

"Have you told Rita?"

"No."

The silence is awkward. It's difficult to untuck my mind from Rita's secret, but I don't want to think about anything apart from Dean.

We carry on walking in the speckled street lights. There's no one else around. It's only us.

"Do you think we're the only ones left?" I whisper. "That they've all gone, apart from us?"

"Gone where?"

"I don't know. Just away."

Dean's laugh drifts steady around us.

"We've got the whole world to ourselves," he says.

As we cross the grass, I bend down to feel the dew on my palms and bring the wet to my forehead.

"A strange place to wash your face," Dean says.

"Lil says it's water left by fairies."

Dean smiles at me. "I've missed you," he says.

"You have?" But he only nods and looks down at his trainers in reply.

We walk together to where the skate park starts and the ground turns hard and gray in the moonlight. Dean runs to the top of the closest ramp and his board thuds soft as he drops it flat. He stands on it, bends his knees low and sails fast down. He's somewhere else for these seconds. Somewhere I can't see. At the top of the other side he jumps so high that my dad wouldn't even be able to touch him, before he spins his way back to me.

"Ready to try?" he asks.

"If I break my arm and can't perform, Tricks'll kill me."

"You'd better not break it then. We'll start here." He takes my hand again and we walk away from the ramp, to where the ground is completely flat and ends in a small, blackened dip. Dean kicks the board to my feet. "Right, it's all about balance, so you'll be fine. I'll run alongside you the first time."

It feels unsteady, as if the whole ground is moving. Dean holds my elbows and starts to walk and then run.

"Don't let go," I say.

"I won't." There's the sound of his feet next to me, the soft tumbling of wheels spinning. Dean moves down with me, and I think I'll topple off the front but he keeps me steady until we're going up the other side onto the flat again.

"Easy." His smile is so bright in the almost-dark.

"I'll try it on my own," I say.

"You sure? Your dad will have even more reason to hate me if you get hurt."

"He doesn't hate you." But the word whittles far too strong at me. "He just doesn't know you."

"And if he did?"

There's silence and darkness and a million barriers between us.

"You're a flattie."

"Is it really that bad?"

"It's all he'll ever see."

I can't bear that Dean knows what that means, so I push off with my foot before he can stop me, stand steady with the cold night holding tight. At the edge of the dip I have the briefest second of regret, before speed snaps at my arms, my face and the sound of the wheels takes me downward, adrenaline fixing quick to my bones.

I fly up the other side and jump off at the top, the board leaving me to skate to a stop on its own.

"You did it!" Dean's shout gets closer as he runs along the top of the ramp toward me.

"Of course I did," I laugh. "I'm a circus girl."

"My circus girl." He picks me up and swings me around. His arms feel different but safe. I want to spread my hands wide under the moon, but instead I hold him close.

And suddenly he kisses me. Dean kisses me. His lips are on

mine, and his hand is gentle on my cheek. Around us, the skate park watches silently as I kiss him, my boy from the fountain. It plants stars in my blood, dizzy ones that feel like they've lost their way. And I never want it to stop.

But he pulls away and looks at me. "What are we going to do?" he asks.

"We'll find a way," I say, more confident than I feel.

Dean puts his arms around me and holds me so close, my circus-girl heart beating into his. He kisses my forehead, breathing me so that I'm a part of him.

"Let's go on the board together," I say.

"You really do want your dad to hate me." He laughs, but the word is harsh against my skin.

"I won't break anything," I say. "It'll be good." I keep his hand in mine and lead him to the board, kicking it straight underneath us.

"You're serious?" he asks.

"Yes. You step on too."

"But not down the ramp," he says, as he holds me closer.

"Don't be scared, or we'll fall," I say.

The space is tiny, but I push off with my foot. I lean to make it turn a bit and Dean instantly knows where we're heading.

"Laura." But I don't let him jump off. Instead, I kiss him. The skateboard falls forward down into the bowl, running away with us on it, the swoop of it stealing my stomach for a split moment.

Suddenly we rock and spill from the board as we go up the ramp, Dean tripping but standing and holding me from hitting the ground.

"You OK?" he asks, but he's laughing, his eyes alive.

"I'm fine."

"I think I should get you back before you break any bones."

"Do we have to go?" But I know he's right. The darkness is being edged into morning, and we can't risk someone catching us together. I hold his hand tight as we walk away.

The wall next to us drops lower, enough for us to see a sparked line of the sun pressing above the horizon. I wish we could stop and watch it rise. I want to kiss Dean again as the sky turns itself blue. But instead we start to sprint across the grass, Dean's board held close in his other hand. We only slow down when we see our site, the striped big top rising like a fire in the middle of our vans, clearer now in the new light.

"Will you come and see me again?" I ask, stopping to look at him.

"Of course."

"Tomorrow?"

"It'll have to be early."

"How early?"

"I'll be here at five."

"Five? What is it with you and mornings?"

"I want to take you to a place I go."

"I'll meet you here then."

I want so much for him to kiss me, but I know there could be anyone watching.

"Are you OK to get back to your van?" he asks.

"It's literally just there," I smile.

"OK." He hesitates. "I'll see you tomorrow."

And he turns and runs away from me, back to where he must have parked his car.

My smile is still wide and safe as I go around the corner of our big top. But Dad is standing by his van.

"Inside," he says when he sees me. His sharp tone makes me too shocked to argue and I go past him and up the steps.

Ma is standing by the sink.

"Where've you been?" she asks. I want to ask her why she's awake so early and what does she really care, but Dad's anger is boiling beside me.

"I was out," I say.

"That's obvious," Dad says, closing the door to the outside world. "Ma needed some air and she saw you sneaking off in the dark. Where did you go?"

"Just out."

"With Dean?"

Dad saying his name makes my mind loop in panic.

"Who?" I ask, although I know it'll only make things worse.

"Do you take us for fools?" Ma asks.

"No."

"How long did you think you could hide him from us?" Dad asks.

"I'm not hiding him."

"So you just forgot to tell us?" It's the disappointment in Dad's eyes I look away from, my cheeks burning red. "You're to stay away from him," he says.

"But there's nothing wrong with him," I say firmly, even though inside my nerves are beginning to split and fray.

"Of course there's not," Ma says. "You know it's not that."

"You don't have relationships with them," Dad says.

"You can't say that," I tell him.

"I can. I'm your dad, and you're part of our family, our way of life, and these are the rules."

"You'll wake Gramps," I say.

"Leave Gramps out of it," Dad says, but he's quieter now.

"He's worth it," I say. I mustn't cry. "He's different to the rest."

"How many of the rest have you known?" Dad says, his voice thrown loud again.

"None," I hurry out. "Not in the same way."

"Is this what you've been getting up to? When you go looking around the towns?" Dad asks. Ma puts her hand on his arm.

"Dean is a flattie, Lo," she says. "Being with him is just not possible." She sits down slowly, as though this will help peel Dad's angry words from the ceiling. "And what about Spider? It's always been you and him. He'd look after you."

"You can't choose who you fall for." I glare at her, willing her to hear what I'm really saying.

"Dean won't be good for you," she says calmly. "It's all wrong."

"What do you know about right and wrong?" I say. I feel the words about her and Rob rolling in on a wave and I'm not sure I can stop them.

"Lo," Ma starts, but suddenly she's still. Her face is unmoving, yet behind her eyes the pieces of her secret are coming together too sharp and painful. She knows that I've somehow stumbled on the truth.

"What?" I challenge her. "And why were you even walking around in the dark?"

But she doesn't speak. And all she can do is look at me, panic beginning to lace tight in her eyes.

"Lo," Dad says. "I won't have you talking to your mom like that." I stare at him but keep my lips clamped tight, because I don't trust them not to say something that will break his heart. "I'm going to make this very clear to you." His voice comes toward me. "You are not to see Dean again. Is that understood?"

Silence is my answer as I storm away from them. The slam of their front door behind me isn't loud enough, but it makes me feel better.

I stumble up the steps of Terini and barge into the bedroom.

"Lo?" Rita says, her voice confused by sleep.

"They want me to stop seeing Dean."

"Of course they do."

"I can't."

"They only want what's best for you."

"Don't you wade in." I slump on my bed, facing the wall to block the coming day.

"It's going to hurt you."

"And stopping seeing him won't?"

"Of course it will. But it's the better of the two options."

"He's not just an option, Rita."

"You hardly know him."

"I know enough," I snap at her. "I thought you'd be on my side."

"I'm always on your side."

"Then you need to tell them that I should keep seeing him. You're my big sister, they'll listen to you."

"Dean's a flattie, Lo. He can't keep traveling miles to see you."

"He can."

"OK, and then what? If you want to stay together, do you just leave us all?"

"Maybe," I say, but I'm not sure I mean it.

"And go and live in that town?"

"It's nicer than you think."

"We don't fit there, Lo. In their eyes, we'd forever be travelers, not good enough for them."

"I'm good enough for Dean."

"Of course you are. But it can't work. You won't be happy, not in the end."

"And you will?" Her feelings for Rob hang in my words, but she pretends she can't see them.

"Settling with one of ours is the right thing," she says.

"Rob isn't one of ours," I remind her. But Rita ignores me.

"It's worked for everyone else."

"Has it? What about Ma and Dad?"

"What about them?"

"Are they really happy?" I ask.

"What are you talking about, Lo?"

I could tell her now and stop the wheels of her life as she knows it. Change the course of where we're all going.

"Nothing," is all I say, leaving the truth to burn its way through me.

I hear Rita turn over and pull her duvet tight to her.

"I'm not performing today," I say, although I know I will.

"Don't be daft."

"I'm not."

"You can't not perform just because you feel lovesick."

"I can."

"Well you'd be letting everyone else down, and that's not fair. You're not that special, Lo." Her words feel like she's hit me. "I didn't mean it like that," she says quickly. "But we've all been upset, and we all get over it. You're no different."

For the first time in my life, I feel completely alone. I get up and walk away from her.

"Lo?"

But I ignore her and go into the bathroom. It's warm in here and too small, but I want it smaller, so I can smash through the walls all at once with my hands and feet. Make big, dirty holes to crawl through and run away.

Spider and I sit together in the make-up van. He leans closer to the small mirror balanced on the table, rimming his eyes with deep brown.

"I miss you, Lo," he says.

"I'm right here," I tell him. I look like I'm wearing half a mask, with foundation smeared thick on only one cheek.

"You're not really," he says. "It feels like you've got secrets that are taking you away from me." His sadness sits heavy on me.

"I'm sorry," I say.

"Is it Dean?" he asks quietly.

"A bit," I say.

"Do you love him?" he asks, as he sweeps the soft pencil thick over his eyebrows.

"Maybe."

He's quiet as he puts his make-up in neat lines on the table. I squeeze more foundation from the tube, curling it onto my fingertip, rubbing it thick onto my clear cheek.

When Spider turns to look at me, I realize how much I've missed him too.

"What's it like?" he asks. "To be in love?"

"It feels like I'm flying through the air, but the trapeze is out of reach, so I just keep flying."

Spider smiles. "Typical Lo."

"You'll find it one day too, Spides," I say steadily. He looks down, brushes something from his leg that's not there. "But it won't be real if you're not honest with yourself."

"It's easy for you to say." His voice is so quiet I barely hear it.

"None of it's easy. Me being with Dean isn't easy. But it's about knowing what you want and being brave."

"Maybe I'm not brave."

"You are." I reach out and hold his hand tight. "You walk over burning coals and lie on beds of knives."

"That's different."

"No it's not. Every day you step from a ledge and walk across a wire. If you're brave enough to do that, you're brave enough to speak the truth. Everyone would still love you, Spider."

"How can you be sure they would?"

"Because you're Spider. And you're brilliant."

He looks up at me, the greasepaint making his eyes sparkle.

"Promise me," I say. "That one day, you will."

His smile hesitates, but it's real. "Just for you, Lo. I promise."

★ ★ ★

White mist takes me, the changeling, into the center of the ring. I'm alone, but I know I'm being watched. The *corde lisse* hangs down, the thick rope being my chance to escape. I hold it and pull myself upward, twisting it with me as I go.

Music washes gentle over us all as my hands grasp me higher. My back bends until I face the floor far below, the smoke still drifting toward me. There's the familiar pull in my muscles as I stretch my legs out, my arms and stomach burning strong to keep me safe.

There's nowhere like this. Where I feel free, yet am trapped by hundreds of eyes and caught breaths.

I climb so high that I mustn't fall, closer to my home, curling my body, twisting it out, my hands gripped tight. And as I hang, split steady in the air, I wonder if Dean is watching, if he's here.

Beneath me, figures appear. Ernest, Spider, Ash, their faces painted with hollow eyes and bleeding lips. In this scene, they are changelings who've stayed on earth, grown bitter and worn and waiting to drag me with them.

The music changes, suddenly pounding into the air. To escape, I must go up. The rope curls around my body. Higher, away from them, taking the cloud-swing from their reach.

But the changeling loses her grip and tumbles. I close my eyes but count and feel as the world unravels, until I let go.

They catch me, as I knew they would, and place me carefully in the disappearing mist, before I run to the ring door curtain, hooked open by Gramps, which swallows me whole.

Chapter Eight

LO

I wake up as a ringing sinks sharp into me. Under my pillow, I hurry to press down the button on the alarm.

"Rita?" I whisper.

"What was that?" So it woke her. She's moving in the bunk above me, and I imagine her sitting up, her eyes still shut foggy with confusion.

"It's nothing. Go back to sleep."

"But what was it?"

"I'm just going to meet Dean." I'm hesitant to tell her. She hated feeling Dad's anger rolling around us yesterday, spreading even into the performance where his face seemed chipped from stone.

She stays silent as I step from my duvet into the cold and reach for the pile of clothes I folded neat under my bed last night. It's easy to get dressed in the dark, to find my pillow and slip my night T-shirt underneath.

"I don't think you should go," Rita finally says.

"I thought you'd gone back to sleep."

"I'm serious, Lo. You'll get hurt."

"Dean won't hurt me."

"The situation will."

"That's a big word for you." She can't see me smile as my hands pad the air to find her. On tiptoes, I lean over and kiss her head. "I won't be long," I say as I put on my coat. "I'll be back for breakfast." At the door I look to where I think she must be.

"Don't tell anyone."

The air is like a web on my face as I close our front door slowly behind me.

"Laura?" It's Dean. He's here waiting, as he said he would be. For a few seconds, I forget everything but him. The way he stands, his hands in his pockets, his coat zipped up against the early cold.

In this moment, I'm happy.

I jump from the steps so no one hears them make a noise.

"Hey," I whisper as I go to him and feel his hand in mine.

"Ready?"

"Yes," I say, even though my mind is still muddled in dreams. We walk across the grass, Dean and I, quickly crossing the street from the circus site and its sleeping windows.

"This is it." The car doors click too loudly as Dean opens them. "Sorry about the mess," he says as we get inside. It makes me hold my breath a bit, the biscuit wrappers and paper scattered on the floor. I stop myself from running my finger through the dust on the dashboard. My mom would have a fit if she saw it.

"Are you going to tell me where we're going yet?" I ask, as Dean starts the car and we join the empty road.

"No," he replies. "Sorry it's a bit cold. The heater will work better in a minute."

"That's OK."

It feels strange to be in here, alone with Dean, going further away from what I know. In the wing mirror I see our white vans beginning to take shape in the lightening dark. I feel suddenly sad as they get smaller, before we turn right and they disappear.

A car drives past. The woman doesn't even seem to see us as she curves away along the road.

"Where do you think she's going?" I ask.

Dean shrugs. "Anywhere."

Anywhere. She can just get in her car and drive away.

"I'd like to do that," I say.

"You drive around all the time. Going to new places," Dean says.

"It's different, though. I may as well be on a track with my eyes closed."

"Maybe you should open your eyes then."

"That's easy to say when flatties are free to do whatever they want."

"You really think that?" Anger creeps slightly into Dean's voice. "My mom is chained to her jobs. If she stops, there's no money."

"She's still free to live where she wants."

"No, Laura. She's completely trapped in her life."

Guilt ticks quick into me. I'm so wrapped up in my mom and Rob and Rita's foolish dream that I'd forgotten Dean's world.

"Is she already at work?" I ask, trying to make it right again.

"She left hours ago." For all these years, his mom has been working while we're all asleep. When it's neither night, nor morning. When time somehow falls into the crack in between.

"She'll come back tired and then still have to go out to clean someone else's house. It's why I have to stick at this college course. I've got to get a good enough job to help change her life."

"You should be studying art, though." It's been on my mind, how this boy with freedom at his fingertips isn't going where he'd choose.

"There's no money in that."

"Money isn't everything."

"It is when you haven't got it." He stares straight ahead, not even glancing at me. "You know, it's not all roses outside of your circus."

"What do you mean?" There's something unsettled between us, and I don't know how to sort it.

"Normal life is tougher than you think. Some people would give anything to have what you've got." His voice isn't harsh. But it's got truth weaving in and out of the words and it makes me feel more lost than ever.

We don't talk any more, but slowly the silence loses its edge. I like the quiet, it helps settle the confused noise messy in my head.

We drive until the buildings become further apart and the fields and trees take over. Until the sky is no longer completely dark, as morning pushes against it.

Eventually we turn down a rickety track where hedges stack up either side.

"Nearly there," Dean says.

"Nearly where?"

"I want to show you the starlings."

"The what?"

"The birds. Starlings."

"Starlings? You better not have dragged me out of bed for nothing."

"I haven't." But already it's been enough. Just being next to Dean, my mind peaceful. "It's amazing. Honestly."

He stops the car in a space at the side of the track, and when he turns the engine off real silence appears. For a moment, we don't move, but then Dean is unclicking his seat belt, opening his door.

"Come on. We don't want to miss it."

We get out of the car and Dean holds my hand as we cross over to the other side.

"Careful here," he says, holding back a bramble, and I follow him to where there's a thin break in the sharp bushes. At the end there's a fence and Dean kneels down, lifting the wire high enough for me to crawl through.

"Sorry. It's not exactly elegant," he says. If Ma could see me now, scraping my knees, my clean palms pressed flat to the earth.

Dean clambers through after me, all legs and arms pushing through the wire as I hold it open for him.

"Quick," he says. He takes my hand again and we run over the bumpy ground, across a wide-open field.

"What if a farmer shoots us?" I've read it in books, I've heard it in the songs Dad sang to us as children.

"There aren't any farmers," Dean laughs. "It's just a nature reserve."

"A what?"

"For people to walk around, look at the animals and plants and everything. It's too early so it's closed now, which means everyone misses the best part."

He keeps hold of my hand as we wade through the long grass, with stalks almost white where they brush against us. The sky is rushing to get light. Here, the new day feels like a whole new world, the trees behind us pushed strong through the ground in the night, the sky painted on for the first time. I could live here. Stay here. Grow my own home up from the earth and have its bricks hold it steady.

"Look." Dean sounds like an excited child as he pulls me down to crouch next to him. "There." He's pointing to the land moving in front of us.

"What is it?" I whisper.

"Starlings." He looks at me, his eyes bright. And I see now, the tiny feathered bodies swaying together.

"But there are hundreds of them."

"Thousands. Watch. It won't be long."

"What won't?" But as I say it, a few of the starlings lift gentle from the ground. Within a second, they all follow, a rush of thousands and thousands of wings swooping them up. I can hear their feathers, a heavy rumble as they rise higher. Suddenly, they all turn together, as if they all just know.

"How did they do that?"

"They're amazing, aren't they?" Dean only glances at me before he's back watching them. They peak at the top, then shoot down so low. A smudge of paint thrown dripping into the sky.

"I love it," I whisper, although I hadn't meant to speak.

"I knew you would," Dean says.

The racing black cloud suddenly bends and twists, changing color from black to gray. They're like nothing I've ever seen, nothing I knew existed, these tiny black stars meeting to make a whole. I feel so small, but as big as the world all at once.

"They remind me of you," Dean says.

"Of me?" I don't take my eyes from the starlings. I don't want to miss any of it. Any of the shapes of their dance.

"The way they move like it's impossible," Dean says. "The way you fly, in your circus."

So this is what the audience sees. Now it's my breath held as I watch them leap and twist symmetrical in the air. Our eyes watch them, so they won't fall.

I hold Dean's hand and I know.

"My own circus," I say.

"All for you."

Thousands of feathers fold and beat against the bodies above us, knowing exactly what to do. Our circus birds, bending in the white.

"Look," Dean says. He's pointing to the edge of the group, to a bigger shape tracking them closer. "A hawk."

"Is it trying to get them?" But I know it is. It's waiting for its time, for a mistake, for a starling to forget its way and lose the others.

"I think it's why they stay so close together," Dean says.

"So the hawk can't get them."

All I can see now is the hawk hovering.

"Do you think some of them are tired?" I ask. "That they want to stop, but they have to keep following?"

"Maybe."

The sun rises higher and I close my eyes and pretend that this is it, this is all there is. There are no shattered families, just me and Dean, in a field of grass, with a sky filled with starlings.

I hear Dean move beside me, and then he's kissing me. And all the pain goes. He kisses away the past and the future. It's only now, it's all I need. There's the sky above and the ground holding us steady, and I disappear into him. We kiss until everything else tips off the edge of the earth and all that's left is us, in our starling field.

We kiss until we have to stop, and Dean pulls away.

"We can't stay here all morning."

"I wish we could."

"So do I." I'd stay here forever with Dean, away from the burnt edges of my life.

He leans down and kisses me again and everything shrinks to just us.

"But my mom won't be too happy if I'm late for college." And so we go, leaving the starlings behind us.

Dean parks his car away from the circus site, and even though it's still too early for most people to be awake, we walk a wide circle along the beach.

"Best avoid them," Dean says, pointing to a couple close together by the beach huts.

I can tell who it is straight away. I start to drag Dean back where we came.

"What is it, Lo?" he asks.

But anger roars so loud in me that it blocks everything else out. It blocks out the sea, the sky, the sand and replaces it all with Ma's skin on Rob's. I let go of Dean and start to run.

Somewhere, I'd been holding onto the hope that Spider and I had got it wrong. That it hadn't been my mom after all. Or maybe she'd just been showing Rob something, a mark on her skin that made her take her shirt off. I'd imagined all sorts of excuses and hadn't realized that I'd been hanging onto them all.

But now she's sneaking off with him again. My dad will be waiting for her, while she's running fast away, not caring if she breaks us.

Dean pulls me to a stop. I'm breathing hard. I feel like spilled petrol, ready to burst into flames.

"What's wrong, Lo?"

"It was Ma and Rob," I say and he can't hide the shock on his face. "I hate her."

"You don't. Not really."

"I do." And I'm crying in front of him, but I don't care. Because everything's twisted and it hurts too much to hold it in.

"You're going to be OK," he says.

"How?" I cry. Dean puts his arms around me.

"Because you're strong."

"But I hate her," I say, staring hard at him.

"You've got to try not to. It's not worth it. It just makes everything more complicated."

He gently pushes my hair from my eyes.

"How am I going to go back?" I ask. "How am I supposed to live with them? And do today's shows with Rob, when I want to kill him?"

"You'll do what you did yesterday and before that. You'll get through it because you have to."

"And tomorrow and after that?"

"Yes."

"Until it explodes and the secret will kill us all?"

"It won't kill you," he says.

"But it feels like my life has capsized, Dean."

"You can't change what she's done, Laura. The only person who can make it right is your mom."

"But what if she doesn't? What if the whole boat just completely flips over?"

Dean looks at me steadily. "Then you swim."

RITA

I can hear Lo shouting as I walk across the grass. I run up the steps of Mada and the argument flies toward me as soon as I open the door.

"I don't have to," Lo screams. I don't ever remember seeing her like this, not this bad. It makes me hesitate, scared to touch her.

"You do," our mom says. She's standing still and her voice is strong.

"You can't make me."

"You'll be letting Rita down." Ma nods at me, as though I've always been in here and a part of Lo's wild anger.

"What's going on?" I ask, staying by the front door. I don't want to go in any further. I think I'll melt from Lo's rage.

"I'm sick. So I can't work tonight." Her anger has turned to tears.

"Not too sick to shout at me," Ma says.

I go to Lo, because she hasn't. Even though Lo's crying, Ma hasn't rushed to her like she should, like she normally does.

"Ma," I plead.

"We can't do the show without the changeling," Ma says. I've heard her voice like this before. It's as though she's put a big full stop at the end of her words.

Lo stands up and runs from their van, slamming the door so hard that the pictures on the wall rattle.

I follow my sister into Terini and slowly close the door behind me.

"Lo?" I don't know why I whisper. Maybe because the

sound in Mada was too strong and I need to balance it out. I don't know if she hears me. She's curled tight on top of her duvet, the pillow over her head, her tears digging deep into her sheet.

"Lo. It's me." I sit down next to her and she takes the pillow away. Her hair is plastered scraggy all over her face. She doesn't bother to push it away.

"What's wrong? Is it Dean?"

"Why does it always have to be about Dean?" She sits up suddenly and I think she'll start shouting again. "Can't you see that he's the one thing keeping me happy?" She pushes past me, swings our bedroom door wide and stamps to the bathroom. I hear her lock herself in.

★　★　★

"What's wrong with Lo?" Spider asks. "She looks like she's been crying." On the other side of the ring door curtains, the buzz of the audience reaches through.

"She's just feeling a bit ill," I tell him. "She didn't want to perform, but Ma says she has to."

"Something else is wrong," Spider says. "You're being weird."

"It's nothing."

I watch my mom and dad through the crack in the curtain. She passes him an armful of knives, which he starts to juggle, tapping them on his knees, his elbows, clutching one in his mouth. The people watching clap to the music. Dad takes the sticks of fire from Ma. He throws them high, so that they turn in the air, spinning by each other until he catches them all. He doesn't burn his skin. He never does.

My mom wears her smile fixed proud, fluttering around him as Dad does his bow and they run back past us through the curtain.

"I won't drop you," Ash says, before we move out together, our skates' wheels spinning down the path Rob has set up for us. His angel wings touch mine as we step onto the wide podium, hold each other's wrists tight and begin to spin. I concentrate on his face as the music takes our wheels and moves them faster.

Everything around us streaks in color. Ash nods enough for me to see and I jump into him, twisting my legs so that he has hold of my ankles. When I throw myself back, the audience gasps together over the music. It's this I love. The tight knot of adrenaline slowly loosening and spreading down my arms to my toes.

Ash spins fast and begins to dip me down and up, my hair flying backward, my arms tucked to my sides. He swings me closer to the floor, but I trust him. He lifts me high above the level of his head and straight down to the floor as we spin, so fast that I have to close my eyes to stop the dizziness from sinking too deep.

My head is so close to slamming into the floor. If Ash makes a mistake, I wonder if my skull will actually crack. Would everyone see my secret thoughts spilling out?

He starts to slow down, and he lifts me, twists me around again so that I'm sitting on his shoulder. We wave to the faces with their wide eyes, watch their hands clapping to the beat of the music as we step off the podium and skate away from them.

★ ★ ★

"Are you sure Lo's not sick?" Ash asks. Dad and Spider carried our barrel fire down to the beach and the sticks inside are beginning to turn into flames.

"She just didn't want to come," I say. Dad is talking to Tricks, but he's near enough to hear my words.

"Does she need to see a doctor?" he asks, as Spider stands up and settles a long piece of driftwood into the barrel.

"It's too damp to light," Stan tells him, but Spider leaves it there, sticking out of the top.

"She's fine. She just wanted an early night."

It's too dark to see the sea, but I can hear it folding its waves and tugging at the sand.

"That's not like Lo," Ash says. But I wish he'd leave it.

"Maybe she wanted a change," I say, sharp enough to try to stop him asking more.

Dad laughs gently at something Tricks says and moves up to make room for Stan.

"Rob says he saw her with that Dean again," Ash says quietly, so only I can hear. I'm trying to think of an answer. "That he saw her getting into his car."

"Is he spying on her?" I say light-heartedly, trying to keep out the trickle of jealousy that Rob told Ash and not me.

"So does Lo think he's going to come and see her in the next town and the next?" Ash asks.

"I don't know," I answer.

"It can't work," he says.

"Then you don't need to worry about it."

"What about Spider, though? She should think about him," Ash says.

"I'm going to go and check on her," I say, getting up.

"Don't be angry with me, Rita," Ash says.

"I'm not," I say. "I'm worried about Lo, is all." And I bend down to kiss him on the cheek, to let him know that we're family and we always be.

I regret wanting to leave as soon as I stand up, as I see Rob stepping over the low wall and walking toward us. I try to pretend that I don't feel it in my stomach, that him getting closer doesn't make my heart beat faster.

"Off to bed already, Rita?" he asks as he stops next to me.

"Yes," I say.

"That's a shame."

I hold his words close to me as I walk away.

Chapter Nine

LO

There's no sign of last night's barrel fire, not even a charcoaled stick to give it away. Dean is waiting by the edge of the sea, where he said he'd be. He's wearing a different coat, a warmer one to keep out the cold.

"You're early," he smiles as I get to him.

"So are you."

He bends down and kisses me on the lips. But he looks nervous, too close to the edge of my world.

"Are you OK?" He leans his head a bit to the side. The early sun is in line with my eyes as I look at him.

"Not really," I say.

"Do you want to talk about it?" he asks, but I shake my head. Rita, Ma, and Rob are trying to take over my thoughts, but I won't let them.

"Can we walk a bit?"

He nods. "I made something for you." He holds my hand, and I let him lead me.

Further up the beach, there're shapes in the sand.

"Close your eyes," Dean says and I laugh as I do.

"What is it?" I ask as we edge further forward.

"OK. Open them."

In front of us, hundreds of tiny sand starlings swoop in their yellow sky. Some cling to the edge of a trapeze scooped and molded from the grains.

"Do you like it?" He seems uncertain.

I know I'm the girl who sits on the bar, my changeling wings dotted with shells, my eyes made from sparkled sea-glass.

"I love it." I want to say more, that it's the best thing anyone's ever done for me, but my words get lost. Instead, I step closer to Dean and I kiss him. I can taste the salt on his lips as I put my hands into his hair and pull him to me. My anger, my hurting, it all disappears. And in its place there are sand sculptures and stars.

It's seagulls squawking that pulls us apart. We both look up as three of them screech in the sky above us.

"They're challenging us," I say. "To beat the sea."

"To what?"

"To make the waves stand still."

I pull him with me to step over an abandoned stretch of shells and go so close to the sea that it almost touches us. The sand underneath our feet is wet, and I feel the soles of my shoes sink in slightly deeper.

I dare the sea to get me, but Dean grabs my hand and pulls me backward, laughing suddenly. We run toward it again and it almost catches us before it scurries back. And it drags with it everything that's been burrowing into my mind, flinging it all high with its spray.

"Wait till the very last second," I say, Dean's hand still in mine. And we pause like statues until the racing water moves us up the beach.

Dean laughs again and happiness isn't just near him, it's actually in him, taking up all the space.

"It's winning," he says.

"No. We are." And I pull him to the water's edge and wait for it to snatch wet at us again.

"We should leave our footprints," Dean says, running back with me from the sea.

"Together?" I hesitate. It's mine and Rita's ground we're on.

"I'd like to," he says. "So the beach remembers us." And I know I want to.

"Next to your sculpture," I say and he smiles as we walk back to the starlings still hanging in their different air.

I think of all my footprints, over the years. And how this one will forever have Dean next to me.

"OK," I smile. We hold hands, balancing on one foot, our legs touching, as we push our feet into the sand.

"Will the sea get them?" Dean asks.

"Maybe. But that's OK."

We topple forward, grabbing onto each other's arms to stop ourselves from falling. We look back and our footprints are blurred, almost one.

"They're ruined," Dean says, screwing up his nose.

"No, they're just smudged. It makes them better," I say.

"How's that?"

"No one wants perfect." And the sound of the sea fills my ears as Dean kisses me.

* * *

I know as soon as I get close to our site that something is wrong. There's a strange feeling, wrapping its way around the vans. I should run, but I don't want to know.

Ma is standing by the steps of her home, with Helen standing next to her. They don't see me until I'm almost by them.

"What's wrong?" I ask. Ma jumps a bit and stares right through me. "Ma?"

"It's Gramps," she says. I step back when she tries to hug me. It stops her words.

"Your dad woke up and found him this morning," Helen says.

"Found him where?"

"He fell when he was getting out of bed."

"Where is he?" I ask.

"He's in his room."

"Is he bad?"

"Yes," is all Ma says. She's woven to the spot.

"It was just a small fall," Helen says. "He'll be fine."

"How long was he lying there?" I ask.

"I don't know," my mom answers.

"And you didn't even hear him calling?" I glare at her.

"I'd gone for a walk." She tilts her head forward, her fingers twisting in on themselves. "I didn't realize the time."

"So he was hurt, and he needed you, but you weren't there," I say, my voice rising. "He thought you'd forgotten him."

"Your mom is upset enough," Helen tells me.

"Is she?" My words smash up against her.

"This won't help anyone," Helen says.

"I should have been there," Ma says quietly. Her hoop earrings, her painted lips tell me where she was.

I push past her, up the steps, into their van. Inside, it feels different. I run through the silence and open his door.

Oh, Gramps.

He lies under a sheet, his face swollen with a bruise so purple that it sits on top of his skin. Rita holds one of his hands, Dad the other. They barely glance up at me.

"Gramps?" I say. He opens his eyes, but he looks in pain, as though everything hurts.

"Hello, lass," Gramps says.

Dad reaches his hand to me and I go and take it. I stand clumsy and useless by his side.

"He didn't break anything when he fell," Dad says, squeezing my hand. "So that's good."

Rita stares intently at Gramps.

"Shouldn't you go to a doctor?" I ask quietly.

"I'll be fine." But his voice is small. "Just a little knock, is all."

"It looks worse than it is," Dad says.

"You must take him," I say, but Dad holds up his hand to stop me saying more.

"It's his choice," Rita says, as though she's Ma, and it makes me feel even more helpless.

I sit alone by Gramps's bed. He's sleeping, his hand resting in mine. Rita and Dad are eating their breakfast in the kitchen. I can hear the sound of Ma vacuuming, as if she could clean this all away.

He doesn't look like my Gramps. His face is puffy, its color all wrong, the bruise leaking into the pink.

"Gramps?" I say, but he stays asleep, his breathing steady. "I'm sorry Ma didn't get to you when you fell." I hope that he doesn't hear that I'm crying. "And I'm sorry that I wasn't here. I was with a boy," I whisper. "With Dean. I should have told you before." Regret tries to get at me. "I'd like you to meet him."

I want Gramps to reply, to undo the complicated thread knotted too tight inside me. To give me answers for everything I don't understand. But the room just hums quietly.

"I'm scared, Gramps," I whisper, so quietly that even if he was awake I doubt he could hear. "Nothing feels safe anymore."

The door opens and Dad comes in. His face is weary. Deep worry lines spill into his forehead. He stands by me, one arm over my shoulder.

"How is he?" he asks.

"Still asleep," I say, as the sheet rises and falls, with Gramps's heart beating underneath. "None of us were there for him."

"I know."

Outside, you can just see the sea. I imagine Gramps swimming in it, washing away the bruises and the crumpled wrinkles on his skin. A magic water to make him young again.

"He'll be all right though, Lo. He'll be mended before we know it."

I look carefully at him, and I know he's telling the truth. My dad, who holds trust in his palms.

"What happens, Dad, if someone cuts the threads of our family?" I ask quietly.

He looks at me questioningly. "I'd never let them," he tells me.

And I try so hard to believe him.

RITA

"Rob made it for me."

"What is it?" Lo asks.

"It catches bad dreams in its thread before they reach you."

"Why did he make it for you?" She's annoyed as I hang the dream-catcher from the wooden side of our bunk.

"It's not so strange, Lo." I hadn't thought there'd be this burst of anger. "He'll make one for you."

"I don't want one."

"You can share mine."

"I don't want it hanging there where I can see it," she says, and she pulls it down, snapping the string it hung from.

"Lo."

"It's rubbish in any case," she says, throwing it onto my bed. "You can't make good dreams. Even in real life, when you're awake."

"Don't be like this." I want to hug her, but she has a strange feeling snapping around her.

"Don't be like what?" she challenges.

"Angry with everything."

"I'm not."

"I'll hang it here then," I say, climbing up to my bunk. The spider's web of colored string hangs too short from the other side and sits crooked on my pillow. It has to be able to spin to work. The bad dreams might be caught wrong and sneak back toward me.

There's a knock at the door and Ash's head appears.

"You're running late and Tricks is about to explode," he says.

"Let him," Lo says.

When I stand here, in the very middle of our big top, I feel like a pin on which the world spins. It's completely quiet, but it's a different silence when it's filled with stilled people watching. Maybe their hearts actually stop as they wait. Maybe mine does too.

Alone, I place my fairy queen fingers on the waist-high pole in front of me, as music starts to drift like water around me. The top of the pole twists very slightly under my weight, but I steady it and flip my body up until my hands support all of me. Sometimes, I think even this would be enough for them. But now I slowly bend my body until my feet find my shoulders, my face peeking out from my feathered back. I'm a strange creature, a fairy crab ready to grow more limbs and scuttle away.

I stretch my legs up again, split them into a line in the air, all the time my arms keeping me strong. When I bend my legs again, my feet go past my head, find the other pole and plant themselves there, until I flip quickly from them both, a spiral of feathers landing safely on the floor.

They clap, but they expect more. I fold down my feathers, strap them tight, before I pick up the bow and place it firm between my toes. I hold the arrow as again I handstand onto the pole, sliding the arrow between the toes on my other foot.

My legs bend with the bow over my head, and I have to tip my face up high to see. The target is there, the circle with the smaller circle I must hit. There's no music now, only the steady beat of a drum, slowly at first, building until I pull one leg back, stretch the string taut. When my toes let the arrow go, it flies so fast and straight that I hardly see it. But I know it hits dead center as the fireworks streak through the air.

Music reappears and weaves with the audience's cheering. And I hold my bow and wave to them, the fire from them bright in my veins.

Chapter Ten

LO

Outside, it's not fully light, but I creep out of Terini, closing the door so softly that no one will hear. Dean is already waiting and I run to him. I need him to steady the earth, but I know that it's impossible.

Around us, the curtains of the other vans are closed, so I take his hand and we go around the side of the tent, where it's shut with ropes and a padlock. I spin the numbers, until the metal clunks soft out of its lock. I loosen a few of the ropes, just enough for us to crawl under.

Inside, the light is smothered, and the silence is different. The heavy canvas walls hold everything else away. I lead Dean down between the seats.

"It's weird with no one else in here," he says quietly.

We stop at the edge of the circle, the far side dipped in darkness. I want him to say that it's beautiful, but he doesn't.

I step over the small painted wall and Dean follows me. It's strange to have a flattie stepping on our ground.

"Follow me," I say. Dean hesitates. "I'll look after you."

It's cold in here, and I wish I'd brought my coat. I'm used to the lights and the adrenaline to keep me warm.

I undo the rope that holds the ladder in place.

"We're going up there?" Dean points to where it disappears onto the platform high above us. I smile at him and start to climb.

Dean follows me, the rope shaking slightly with his clumsy movements. I see him below, concentrating hard, placing one hand and then the other. At the top, it's easy for me to step onto the platform, but I reach out to help him.

"It's almost as high as the factory roof," he says. It feels muggy up here, without the crowds to crack open the air.

"Don't go too close to the edge," I tell him, but he sits and dangles his legs over the side.

"So this is what you see," he says.

"It's different during a show. There're lights. And a lot of noise."

"Have you ever fallen?" Dean asks.

"Only with the safety net. My grandma died, though. She fell badly during a show when I was little."

"So it's dangerous?"

"It was a freak accident. They can happen anywhere."

"Aren't you scared?"

"No. Performing is as normal as breathing for us. I don't even think about it. And anyway, that's what people like. The more dangerous it is, the more they'll pay." I smile at him. "Do you want a go? On the trapeze?" Tricks would kill me if he knew.

"Really? You'll teach me?"

"If you'd like." I pull the rope and the trapeze comes toward us. I have to unlink it to hold the bar.

"What happens if I fall?" he asks.

I look calmly at him. "You won't." And I pass it to him. "Put your hands here." He places his hands beside mine. "Just pull yourself onto it. Remember, it's only a swing. It doesn't matter how high it is."

He's shaking slightly as he pulls his legs up until he's crouching on the bar. It's difficult to keep it steady with his weight.

"Sit down and hold on," I say. "Ready?"

"Yes."

So I let go and he swings away from me. I hear him make a noise, of shock maybe, but quiet enough so that we're not found. I watch him as the bar holds him through the air. He pulls on the ropes as a child would, his legs stretching straight out in front of him. When he comes back to me once more, I jump. My hands grab the bar where Dean sits and he gasps. When he looks down at me, I can tell that he's frightened.

"What are you doing?" he asks angrily.

"It's OK."

I put my feet on the bar and pull myself up, crouching down opposite him. The familiar swoop of the swing sinks into me as I smile at him.

"You might fall," he says.

"So might you."

And I kiss him. We hold tight to the ropes, our bodies barely touching. The space between us seems to flame, burning away the morning. The hurting disappears among the color of happiness so strong on my skin. We kiss until the air slows down and I remember the trapeze.

"How do we get down?" Dean's smile crowds out everything and I kiss him again. "Seriously, Laura."

"We fly." I stand up, my feet either side of him. "Like this."

And I flip backward. Held by circus spirits, I spin and fall and land soft into the net.

Dean looks down. "Serious?" he asks, his voice barely reaching me.

I nod. "I'll catch you," I laugh, standing unsteady with my arms out wide. Dean waves at me to get out of the way.

"I'll crush you," he says.

So I step off the net, swing gently to the floor and watch him high above me.

"Go!" I say.

He hesitates only slightly before he lets go, his body falling, arms flailing, until the net grabs him, lets him go, grabs him again, until he's still.

"That was awesome," he says.

"You're a natural." It's Rob's voice. He's walking over the top of the seats toward us.

"You were watching us," I spit out angrily.

"You're lucky it was me and not Tricks," he says. "Your head would've been on the block, Lo."

He doesn't realize that I know. I know it all, and it's his neck that Dad will want to slice clean from his neck.

"We haven't met," he says to Dean. "I'm Rob," and he puts out his hand. Dean hesitates, before he shakes it.

"We're not interested," I say.

The shock on Rob's face is genuine. He recoils from my words, before they start to make sense in his mind. I see the clever workings of his face crumble. The pretense of who he is slips slowly from him.

And it hurts me, when I don't want it to. For so long he's been Rob, our family, and now I don't know.

He flounders for something to say, as I take Dean's hand.

We half run down the aisle between the chairs, crawl through the widened gap in the tent and into the clearer air.

"Are you OK?" Dean asks.

"No," I mutter.

But how do I explain that the anger and sadness and confusion is pinching me so hard all over and hurts so much that I don't know how to be.

I've lost who I thought my mom was, I've lost who I thought Rob was, and their secret sits sharp between my sister and me.

"I want to get away," I say. And so I let Dean lead me from it all—from the tent and our van and the beach across the grass, to his car, which he opens and we get inside.

The old factory seems even quieter than before. It's sucked the silence out of the night and is holding it tight in its walls for the day.

We walk up stairs I haven't been on before, where dust is caught solid in the corners and stubs of cigarettes sit like burnt-out stars.

We don't go all the way to the top, instead pushing through a door that leads to another. There's a padlock on it that Dean opens and we go inside. The windows of this room are half covered in gray card, which cuts out some of the sunlight, but the graffiti across the back wall is still bright.

"Did you do this?" I ask, walking toward it.

"It's my mom and me." The sprayed picture has them sitting high up on a cliff, their legs hanging down over the edge. Below them, the rocks turn into spirals of color. Above their heads, a cloud of birds is gathered.

"It's incredible," I say. "Who taught you how to do it?"

"I taught myself."

"I didn't know you were this good," I say and he looks embarrassed. "Seriously, Dean. It's amazing."

A row of spray cans stands in front of the painting. Tiny drips of color have dropped in dots on the floor.

"Do you want a go?" Dean asks, as he bends down to pick up two cans of paint.

"I'll ruin it," I say.

"You can have this wall." Next to us, the rusty white color stretches from floor to ceiling. Dean passes the cans to me. "Or you can choose any colors," he says.

"I can't even draw on paper," I say.

"You can. Everyone can. There's no right or wrong, everyone just draws differently."

"Do I just spray it?" As I speak, I press the nozzle and a puff of color appears on the wall.

"Yup," Dean laughs.

"What shall I paint?"

"Anything that's in your head. It's a good way to get it out."

I press the nozzle again and a clearer circle of dripping blue appears.

"Move it more quickly, so it doesn't bleed so much," Dean says.

I twist my wrist up, with the can held straight, and walk along the length of the wall. I paint a straight line from one end to the other. When I stop, I look up at Dean. We smile at each other.

"It's a start," he says. "Is it the sea?"

"No. It's a tightrope."

I go to the row of cans and find the pink. I want it to be Rita's skin color, but it's bubble-gum bright. I paint her balancing on the thin wire and try to make her face right, but it comes out too big. With the red I do a tipped-up smile.

Next to her, I paint my dad. One leg goes too long, but it doesn't make him fall. He has his arm around Rita, folding a bit into her shoulder. I make my dad smile too. He looks proud, his eyes looking up. I make Gramps sleep on the tightrope, but as soon as he's there with his closed eyes, I want him sitting up. I do a big green arrow from the lying figure and paint my Gramps new, sitting with his legs hanging over the wire, his eyes wide awake, not a bruise on his skin.

I know that Dean is watching. From the edge of me, I see him waiting for where I will take the paint.

It's Ma I squeeze from the can. Sprayed drops of color make her fall from the wire. She's reaching out her hands, but I can't tell whether she manages to grab tight to the rope at the last minute.

I put the can at my feet and look up at my graffiti family.

"Is it your mom?" Dean points to the flailing woman.

"Yes."

"You've drawn her head, but not her face."

"She's looking the other way," I say and he nods slightly.

"Where are you in the picture?"

"I'm not in it."

"Don't you want to be?"

"I don't know."

The disloyalty burns me. They're my family and I haven't painted myself with them. I think I'm going to cry and I don't want to—not here.

He steps toward me, his safe arms holding me tight. And I kiss him, to make all of the rest disappear. I kiss him among cans that have fed out my family's bones, given them colored sticks for arms and smudged red mouths. We kiss in the place where his mom once was, when her dreams were formed of solid lines that led only to good.

"I wish we could go away. Really away." It's Dean who stops us.

"Where would we go?" I ask, when I just want to kiss him again.

"Away from it all," he says. "But we can't."

"We can pretend to."

"That's a stupid thing to say." His sharpness shocks me. "But it is," he insists. "We can't just pretend to be together. I can't just imagine that you're here when you're not."

"You said that nothing is impossible."

"Well maybe this is."

My thoughts stumble. *This? Us?*

"Maybe you could join us? Join our circus?"

"And just leave my mom?"

I look up at him, at this boy who comes from a world where people don't move on, with homes stuck deep in the ground.

"Maybe you could come away with us. Your brother could come back to live with your mom."

Anger is quick on his face.

"Are you serious? You think I could just up and leave?"

"I don't know. Maybe." But already I know it's ridiculous, know that they're words I should never have said.

"Have you listened to anything about my life?" he asks. I don't know where this has come from. This row that's bubbled up and is boiling between us. "And you're not exactly living the life you want to. If it's so easy, why don't you just leave your circus?"

I thought he would steady me, but his words have pushed me from my tightrope, and I start to feel myself topple and fall.

"Dad will flip when he knows I've been with you," I say flatly.

"So that's it, the end of the conversation?"

"Yes," is all I say, a cold disc of worry covering up my other words.

"We just give up? As simple as that?" he says, but I don't answer. "So if I turn up tomorrow, will you even be there?"

"I don't know."

"This is pointless. Let's go." But I'd wanted him to kiss me again, to say that he wanted us to stay.

I don't look again at my painting as we walk out of the room. Dean clunks the small padlock back in place and he doesn't take my hand as we go through the next door, down the echoing stairs and back through the empty window with powdered glass at its feet.

RITA

"Rita?" I can hear Rob's voice faintly through Terini's window. I pull the curtain back slightly and he's standing there. "Can I come in?" he mouths, pointing to the door. I nod and drop the curtain back in its place.

I jump down past the ladder witch, and she sees me in my pajamas, watches as I take them off quickly, swap them for the T-shirt Lo left on her pillow. My bare legs stick out of the bottom. I haven't time to do my hair, but I run my fingers through it as I go to the door, taming it where the night has tumbled it wild.

"Morning," I smile. I don't think I've ever seen him this early in the day.

"Can I come in?" he asks.

Lo said she wouldn't be long, but I step back and let him in and close the door behind him.

He's never been in here alone with me. There's only been times with us all playing cards, squashed clumsily on the floor. I can't see him wanting to sit on the top bunk, so I sit on Lo's bed, our feet side by side on the floor.

"It's about Lo," he says and my heart flickers hard with disappointment.

"What about her?" I try to keep my voice light.

"I need your word that you won't say anything. Not until I've decided what to do."

"OK." *How can he know secrets I don't?*

"She's been with Dean. I caught them. They were mucking about on the trapeze this morning and jumping into the net."

"Oh," is all I say. *We'll never tame you, Lo.*

"You don't seem surprised," Rob says.

"I don't think I am."

"You knew?"

"Not about the big top. I didn't know they were in there."

"But about Dean? You knew she was still seeing him?"

"Yes."

"Your dad will go nuts. He thought she wouldn't see Dean again."

"He doesn't have to know."

"I think I have a duty to tell him."

"A duty?"

"It was really dangerous, Rita. What they were doing. She could have got Dean killed."

"But she didn't." I touch his arm without thinking.

"You know the circus rules. Flatties are out of bounds."

"You were a flattie," I remind him, my words edging toward admitting something I barely understand myself.

"It's different. I'm here now, committed to you all."

"She really likes him, Rob."

But he shakes his head at me. "Our circus is too small, Rita. We can't afford to lose a member, or it'll all fall apart."

"We won't lose Lo," I tell him.

"But what if she decides she really wants to be with him? That she leaves us to live with him?"

"That'll never happen, Rob. Lo's blood is with us."

"Do you think she really believes that?" Rob looking at me makes my breathing too shallow.

"I think so," I say quietly.

"I don't know." He stares down at his shoes, next to my bare feet.

"Have you ever felt like that?" I ask. My heart is beating so hard I think it'll break from my skin. "Really liked someone, when you're not meant to?"

He stops and the room stops and my heart stops too.

When he looks up at me, I'm sure there's something different in his eyes.

"Maybe," he says. And he's so close to me that I lean forward and I kiss him. Rob's lips are on mine, and it's what I've thought about and dreamed about and wanted, but it feels different than it's meant to, than I thought it would, because he's not Ash, and guilt swoops in and clamps so hard around my heart that I don't know how I breathe.

Rob stops us. "Rita," he says, shaking his head hard as though to dislodge the me and him that's somewhere in his mind.

I put my hand on his cheek.

"It's OK," I say, and I lean in and kiss him again. He's not as soft as Ash, or as gentle as Ash, but I know I want him.

"We can't do this, Rita," he says, moving from me.

"We can."

I push Ash far, far away. Because it's Rob I should be with, it's Rob I want to wake up next to me each day.

And so I kiss him a third time, feel his hand resting on my leg, underneath Lo's T-shirt.

"Lo will be back soon," he says. His breath is strange. "I've got to go, Rita."

"I know," I say, but I don't think he wants to. He's standing up, leaning against the ladder. I try not to hear the witch's sharp nails. "I'll see you soon." And he moves away and goes out of the bedroom. I hear him open the front door and then it closes and there's the silence of him gone.

I put my fingers to my lips, where he kissed them.

I'm sorry, Ash.

But I'm so happy that I start to laugh.

I pull Lo's T-shirt long over my knees, tuck myself into the smallest I can go and tip myself onto her bed. I close my eyes, my blood sparkling.

LO

Gramps sits on his chair again, the bruise on his cheek already fading. He's feeding himself slowly, his tray balanced on the blanket on his lap. Tricks bought the fish for us from a hut on the beach. Its salty smell sticks to me, as it flakes between my teeth.

Rita puts down her knife and fork. She looks at me briefly.

"I think I'm in love with Rob," she says. The air snaps.

Dad's fork is on his plate. Ma's hovers midway to her lips.

"What on earth are you talking about, Rita?" Dad says.

"I want to be with Rob," she says.

It's silent, apart from our dad scraping food onto his fork and putting it into his mouth. I watch my mom. She stays sitting upright, but her face is falling apart bit by bit.

"I'm sorry if it's a shock," Rita says. Her smile is beginning to fade, but her eyes are still strong.

"You're being ridiculous, Rita." Anger is beginning to tick through Dad's words. "He's old enough to be your father."

"No he's not." She tries to laugh. "He's only thirteen years older. It's not a much bigger difference than Gramps and Grandma Margaret had."

Gramps has stopped eating. He's watching Rita with wise eyes.

"It's just a childish crush," Dad says determinedly.

"I'm not a child," Rita says.

"Yes you are. You're my child and I've had enough of this nonsense."

"It's not nonsense." Rita is staying so calm, so strong.

"But you're with Ash," Ma says. She doesn't look at me. I know Rita's words will burn her in a different way to Dad and she won't want to see that in my eyes.

"I'm not with Ash, not really." But Rita almost winces as she says it, as though she feels Ash's hurt. "Rob feels the same way about me too," she says, her voice shaking.

Dad slams the table with his fist, hard enough for his plate to lift and clatter. He's so blinded by anger that he doesn't see his wife's breathing split.

"What's that supposed to mean?" he shouts.

"It means that he likes me."

There's betrayal at the edge of Ma's eyes. I think I'm the only one who can see the humiliation seeping out of her bones.

"Your dad is right," she manages to say. "Rob is not the right person for you." Each word must scorch her mouth.

Dad suddenly pushes his plate away.

"Wait," Ma says, grabbing his arm. "Calm down."

"Calm down?" I've never heard my dad shout like this. I think the walls will fall and the ceiling will crash.

"Maybe," says Gramps quietly, "we should try to listen to Rita."

But Dad just glares at him. "I won't hear any more of it," he says.

Ma's face is so white and her hands are shaking.

"This won't get us anywhere," she says, as my sister sits in the center of her storm. Rita's trying not to cry, as Ma gets up and walks quickly toward the bathroom. The door closes with a click behind her.

Dad's ragged breaths fill the space. He looks at me.

"Did you know about this?"

I can only nod.

"Right." He pushes his hands on the table to help himself stand. There's power at the end of his fingertips and I'm scared where this anger will take him. "Wait here." And in a few short steps he's out of the front door.

"Why are you not helping me?" Rita quietly asks me. "Is it because I said you shouldn't be with Dean?"

"How do you know Rob likes you?" I ask, but she only looks at me. "This is worse than being with a flattie," I tell her.

"How? At least I wouldn't need to leave the circus to be with Rob."

The bathroom is close enough for Ma to hear it all. I bet she wishes she could stay in there forever, but she must know she can't as the door opens. She comes out and goes to the sink, fills a glass of water and puts it in front of Rita.

"Where's your dad?" she asks.

"I don't know," Rita says.

"I think he's gone to talk to Rob," I tell her, but she doesn't react. There's a mask across her face, and it's drained her emotions.

"To bring him here?"

"Maybe."

The air feels a tight, twisted mess. I've wanted so long to shake sense into my mom, but now I wish I could run her away from it all.

Dad's feet are heavy up the steps. He storms through the door, his face bruise-red. Rob is behind him, and for the first time ever, I see true fear in his eyes.

Dad stands square in front of him.

"I want you to tell me exactly what's going on," he says.

Rob looks first to Ma. I don't know if he even sees Rita sitting here, needing to disappear.

"What do you mean?" Rob asks, as Ma holds his gaze, her expression cold.

"You and Rita." Dad can barely squeeze the words through his teeth.

"Me and Rita?" A line of relief stretches from Rob to Ma, so taut I could snap it, but Dad can't see.

"She seems to have ideas."

"Ideas?"

"That you're in a relationship."

"That's not what I said." A blush rises fast to Rita's cheeks.

"Then remind me exactly what you did say," Dad says.

"Leave it, Dad." It's almost unbearable watching Rita wanting to escape, so finally I speak.

"I don't think you should talk, since you've been encouraging it."

I've never heard Dad like this, with words so sharp they hurt.

"I haven't been," I say.

"There's nothing to encourage," Rob interrupts. He seems completely confused, looking from Dad to Rita. "I don't know what you're talking about, Ray." And it's enough to make my dad falter.

"Have you ever made my daughter think you could be with her?" he asks.

"Never," Rob says. "Why would I do that?" His face is set so straight in innocence that I begin to wonder where the truth is. He looks at Ma. "You have to believe me." And I see it, as he begs. How somehow he's let his heart truly fall for her. But now she only looks back with disgust in her eyes.

"Rita?" Dad demands, blind to everything.

"I didn't say it was a relationship," she says quietly.

"It?" Rob asks. "What's 'it'?"

"Nothing," she says. She won't look at any of us.

"I didn't want to drag you into it," Rob says awkwardly, "because it's embarrassing for Rita. She's got a bit of a thing for me, Ray. I've had to talk to her a couple of times, you know, make it clear. But I'm absolutely not attracted to her. You have my word."

Rita's looking down at her fingers, picking at the skin around her thumb. I see how she breathes, see the look on her face and instantly I know that her feelings are true.

"I think you'd better leave, Rob," Ma says.

"No, it's all right, we're going," I say. I pull Rita up, and she starts crying as I put my arms around her.

Dad breathes out heavily.

"I think we owe Rob an apology," he says.

"She certainly doesn't," I snap.

"Lo." The echo of his anger is still here, but I ignore him as I pull her from the room, away from Mada, away from it all.

RITA

Lo slams Mada's door hard behind us, and she doesn't let go of my hand as she pulls me with her down the steps.

"You're OK, Rites," she says. I try to make her words flatten my tears, but it doesn't work. We go quickly into Terini, away from gossiping eyes.

"They'll all find out," I say, but Lo just closes our front door and stops to hug me tight.

"They won't, because we won't say anything. And even if they do, then it doesn't matter what they think."

"But I don't want Ash to know." I couldn't bear to see the betrayal in his eyes.

I sit heavily on the floor, and Lo strokes my hair as she lets me cry.

"I didn't make it all up, Lo."

"I know."

She wipes her thumbs under my eyes, and I look at the skin on them, streaked with black.

"You look worse than Lil," she says, and her smile tries to make it all better. When she stops still and looks at me, I know she wants the truth.

"Why did you do it?" she asks.

"You said we can't help who we fall for." My anger is heading at her, at the wrong person.

"But Rob? He couldn't have liked you back. Not like that."

I'm absolutely not attracted to her.

I don't hesitate. "No."

But he kissed me. I remember.

Lo breathes out heavily. "Good."

"What's wrong with me, Lo?"

"Nothing's wrong with you."

"Why didn't he like me then?"

"He's not right for you. That's all. He never has been and he never will be."

"But I really thought I liked him. I thought he liked me." I feel the embarrassment twist up my legs and settle sour in my stomach. "How can I even see him again now?"

"You mustn't care what he thinks. He's not worth it." Lo's eyes are so serious. "He's not really one of us, Rita," she says. "He's just a flattie who joined us. He hasn't got our blood. His circus begins and ends with him. One day he'll disappear, and he won't even look back."

"I don't want him to."

"I know. But he has flattie bones, and he can never change that."

"Like Dean?"

Lo hesitates and looks down. "Yes. Like Dean."

"Has something happened?"

"I don't know. We had a row. He said it was impossible."

"You didn't tell me."

"I didn't know how to." Now I can see it, how the spark has gone from her eyes.

"We don't really know them, do we? Not really?"

"No."

I reach over to hold Lo's hand again.

"I thought I knew Rob. I trusted him," I say.

"So did I."

When I put my head on her shoulder, she rests against me.

"So it's back to me and Ash and you and Spider." I think that she'll at least smile, but I can tell that she doesn't.

"Ash is good. And he'll love you to the ends of the earth," Lo says.

"He will, won't he?"

"It was always right there in front of you."

"I thought I wanted more."

"Love is enough, Rita."

"But not for you and Spider."

She doesn't answer. She just sits still, her hand in mine.

LO

Sarah crouches tiny in a hoop above the tightrope. She shakes the feathers from her human body and they drift like stars to the floor. There's silence as they fall, all eyes watching them float strange in the spotlight.

I'm at one end of the tightrope, and it's time for me to go home. The silver line stretches in front of me as music sweeps in, and I know that I must walk.

The bar in my hands is light and steady. It's the difference between keeping me straight and making me fall. I used to love this. To be so caught, yet so free, balancing between this world and the next. But tonight, it's different. There's something in me that wants to jump, to fly away from it all.

I feel the eyes on me now, looking up as I move forward. Underneath my feet the wire rocks slightly, but I know I'm safe.

When I'm close to Sarah I call to her, and she holds out her hand. But a flash of light shows another hoop, so close I can almost touch it. Rita sits there, her fairy queen costume silver now, weighed with sequins for the end of the show. From the ledge, Spider throws her fire-sticks and they fly lit with flames, spinning through the air. Rita catches them and twists them high above her again, enough time for Tricks to lower Sarah's hoop so fast to the ground that the audience gasps.

She jumps into her parents' arms. They take the feathers from her hair, pass her the rag doll that's been waiting.

I hook the balancing pole to the tightrope and I leap. Just high enough to reach the hoop of the fairy queen, just far enough to get myself home.

Behind the ring door curtains, I let go of Rita's hand.

"I've got a headache," I say. "I'm going to get a drink of water."

"I'll let Ma know you won't be long," she says.

I don't tell her that I'm not coming back for clear-up. If I warn them, they'll make me, and I just need to be alone.

Instead, I run outside, into a rain that batters the feathers in my hair and sticks my performing clothes closer to my body. My thick make-up will smudge, but I don't care. I feel the water sink through my skin and into my empty inside. It fills me up, until it breaks my throat and makes me cry.

I run up our steps and through Terini's door, into a van I don't want to be in. It's part of a family that's broken, but no one can see. I'm alone, watching the cracks get bigger and they reach my head and pulse heavy and thick in there.

Under Rita's pillow I find the half-empty packet of painkillers, a silver slice with raised white dots. Five of the circles are crumpled and empty.

In the kitchen I turn on the tap. The cold water feels warm against my damp skin. I watch the glass as it fills, the line rising higher to the top. I imagine floating in it, the wings of my costume spreading out behind my back. The audience shrinks to standing around the edge, looking at my body nearing the rim.

I press one of the pills onto my hand. It's hard on my tongue and the swallow of water pushes it back. I should stop at two, but suddenly I want to see where their white wheels will take me.

"This is because of you, Rob," I say. "And this." One more.

"And this." These will help dull the pain. These will take it all away.

Rita's packet is empty in my hands. I put it in the bin and go into the bathroom. There are two more packets of acetaminophen. One is full, with ten new pills, the other has six dotted in its silvery paper.

In my bedroom, I sit on my bed.

"This is for hurting my dad," I tell Rob. I drop three into my palm and take them all.

"And these are for telling me I can't see Dean," I tell Dad.

"And this is for giving up on us," I tell Dean, clicking four round circles onto my palm. They are difficult to swallow and they rub against my throat and they make me start to cry again.

There are six pills left and one by one I free them all and drink them back, hardly feeling as they slip past my tongue, the taste too faint to barely notice.

Now, the cut edges of my family will hurt less. And maybe if I'm not here, they won't hurt at all.

I lie down and curl my tears into my pillow. Because Dean is right—I could never really stop still in his house of bricks and he'd fall from our turning wheels. He can't visit, the further away we go. The road will stretch and snap, and he won't find his way to me. I'll never have a house, my garden with roots.

I take the empty packets and hide them in the bin.

In the bathroom, I wash my face in a stream of water. The mirror shows black streaks down my cheeks, which I wipe away with cream and swabs of cotton wool.

I sit on my bed and wait. I don't feel anything. I lie on my back and stare up at the slats above me. How many of my secrets are hidden there? The edge of Rita's sheet is tucked under her mattress. I try to hear the ladder-witch breathe.

I wait to feel sick, to vomit the pills back up, but it doesn't happen.

And I start to laugh, too loudly into the silent room. I turn on my side and pull my pillow to my face. I laugh so much that it's difficult to breathe, and I wish that Rita was in here too. I want to hear her laughter right now, to string alongside mine.

But she's not, and the loneliness falls like a blanket and it stops my mouth tight.

I wait for sickness, for something, but nothing comes. The pills have dissolved, they've gone, but they haven't taken me with them.

Chapter Eleven

LO

I wake up and the morning is at the edge of the curtains. I'm under my duvet, in my costume. And I remember.

I run a nail along my skin, and I can feel it. And I can feel my heart thudding into my palm. There's the sound of Rita sleeping above me.

Did I take those pills last night? It feels like my real mind stopped and something else took over. If I had found more pills, would I have taken them?

Did I really, really not want to wake up? Not ever?

Rita would have woken this morning and called to me and I wouldn't have answered. She would have jumped down from her bed and found me.

Guilt pushes hard on my chest. But relief pulls at me. I want to take last night and break it into little pieces that I'll never see again. Because I didn't want to die. I don't know what I wanted, but I didn't truly want to disappear. Not forever.

Quietly I get up, take off my feathered costume, and put

on my night T-shirt. I go from our bedroom, unlock the front door and walk barefoot down the silent van steps. I run across the morning grass, the air light on my skin. I'm over the small wall and on the beach, the sand gritty and cold between my toes. Sharp seaweed catches my ankles as I run.

The sun is fierce and small in the sky, painting shining starlings on the surface of the sea, gathering into a bright streak of line toward me.

The water is freezing on my skin and whips hard at my breath, but I don't want to stop. The cold bites around my knees and tries to push me back, but I dive light above the gentle waves, close my lungs and plunge into the salty green.

Ice pain in my head stops my body tight, and I gasp into the white sky, my feet sinking into wet sand, the block of cold encasing me as I kick through it, feeling it all.

I didn't know that I would swim today and feel like this. I'm alive. The pills didn't work and my relief is as big as the ocean.

I lie on my back, the sea pulsing into my bones. My bones that belong to me and no one else. I move my arms up and down, making an angel shape. And I laugh, knowing that the dot of sun will keep rising in the sky and today I'll be able to face everything and see it all.

My T-shirt is heavy as I splash clumsily from the water, my wet hair like icicles. I run back home slowly, weighted down with cold, but there's a miracle in the sand too and in the colors of the low brick wall, the hard tarmac of the path. And the grass I walk on.

The van still seems to be sleeping. Quietly I open our bedroom door.

"Where have you been?" Rita whispers.

"To see the sea," I laugh.

"You feeling better then?" She turns to face the wall, pulls her knees up tight.

"Much," I say.

"Dad was furious that you missed clear-up last night," she says. "He wanted to wake you up, but Ma said he had to wait until today."

"I better go before he gets up then," I say, rubbing a towel over my hair.

"Go where?" She sits up.

"Only for a bit," I reassure her. "I'm meeting Dean."

"I thought it was over."

"So did I. But I don't want it to be."

"We need you to help pack up."

"I have to see him again, Rita. I won't be long."

"Dad will go mad."

"He'll be OK."

"He won't, Lo. You know it. He'll go nuts." The headache from the cold sea has settled in me, but I can't tell Rita, in case she looks for the acetaminophen and finds them gone.

"What's the worst he can do?" I say. We both know that he'll shout until his face purples, but he'll never do more. "Dean makes me feel alive, Rita."

"And we don't?" She seems so sad and I want to tell her that she mustn't be. That Gramps says things always work out, that the sun rises every day.

"It's different," I say.

I can tell she's hurt, but I haven't time to explain. I get dressed quickly and creep quietly from the room.

Dean's car is around the corner, where it usually is.

"Hey," he says, as I get in. But he sounds nervous, as though maybe he shouldn't be here. He doesn't kiss me. Instead he's already started the car, quick to escape.

"I thought you might not come," he says, concentrating on the road.

"Well I did."

"Are you still angry with me? About what I said?"

"A bit."

"I didn't mean it. We'll work something out."

I smile over at him. But guilt weaves in and out of my veins again, because I nearly left him. And Dad and Ma and Rita. I would have left them all. But now it doesn't make sense. Looking at Dean, at his face, his hands on the steering wheel. How could I have risked losing it all? The pills were a strange crack of time where I thought everything was wrong. But it wasn't true, because I'm alive.

My head pounds at the thought of it. A deep, cold headache that I deserve because I didn't see. I nearly took my sixteen years and snapped them shut. Shame spreads through me like fire.

"What do you want to be?" I ask, needing to see beyond now, to a future I nearly stole.

"When I grow up?" he laughs. "I wouldn't mind being with you." He seems embarrassed suddenly, as though they were words he meant to only think.

"As a job, a career."

"I'd like to be an artist." He says it quickly, as though it's the first time he's dared to let the words out.

"You're good enough," I tell him.

"Do you think?"

"I know it."

"But I'd want to be one that breaks boundaries. Maybe a secret one, like Banksy."

"Who's he?"

He glances over at me. "Do you really not know?"

"Why would I?"

"He paints amazing pictures on walls all over the world. Like graffiti, but better. He makes people see things differently."

"He sounds brilliant."

"He is. His paintings sell for loads of money now."

"You could be like him. And you could earn enough money to build us a house. We could have a garden, and I could grow my tomatoes."

He glances at me and nods.

"You have more options than I do," I say. "I only know the circus."

"You could do anything, Laura, if you wanted to enough."

"You really think that?"

"I know that."

He reaches over and briefly holds my hand.

"We'll be OK," he says.

"We have to be," I tell him. Because we do.

"Your dad's going to be even more angry with me now, though, taking you for a drive when you should be there."

"He shouldn't have put up barriers then," I say. Although thinking of his disappointment makes my chest hurt and my heart beat too quick. It makes my palms sweat and the pounding makes my head hurt more.

"Are you OK?" Dean looks at me strangely.

"I feel like I'm going to pass out," I say.

"Put your head between your knees," he says, but it makes the pain whistle deeper into my skull. "Take some deep breaths." He opens the window and I breathe invisible droplets from the sky and it helps clear my lungs. My beating chest begins to steady. "There's some water in the back."

I reach behind me for the bottle. I open it and the drink is cool on my tongue.

"It's made my headache worse," I say.

"It's because it's cold," he says. I screw the lid back on and drop it on the floor of the car. "Do you think I should take you back home?"

"Maybe."

So Dean turns the car around and keeps glancing at me. "Were you feeling ill before?" he asks, his forehead a knot of worry.

"No."

"Do you think it was a panic attack then?" he asks.

"I don't know." I rest my head against the back of the seat and close my eyes.

"We need to talk to your dad," Dean says. "If it's making you feel like this, we need to show him that I'm all right and he's got nothing to worry about."

"You're a flattie," I say simply.

"But you can't go getting sick because of it."

"I know." I move my head against the window, hoping that the cold glass will somehow soothe the sharpness in my head. But it doesn't.

Dean stops the car close to the circus field. Even from here I can see my dad standing outside the van, his face buried in anger.

"I'm not sure I can do this," I tell Dean.

"You can. You have to. You can't just never go back."

"Will you come with me?"

"Now?" Dean runs his hands over the steering wheel. Dad spots us. It feels like a net has fallen onto the car.

"No. You'd better go," I say.

Dean looks at me, and I want to kiss him, but Dad's eyes are boring into us. Instead I touch his hand and I hope that it's enough.

"When will I see you?" he asks, his fingers holding onto mine. But Dad is walking toward us, his strides big and heavy.

"Soon."

"Are you going to Thetford next?"

"Yes." And I have to let him go.

I open the car door, step out onto the pavement, and start to walk away. I hear the engine start, and I know that Dean is leaving.

My legs are shaking, and my dad is almost here. I'm waiting for him to bellow the sky down, but he doesn't. Instead, he comes right up to me, his face a hard mask of anger.

"Where were you?" he asks.

"I went out with Dean."

"That's clear," he says.

"I wanted to see him before we move on."

"First last night and now this."

"I'm sorry." There are clouds above us, but it feels like bright sun is pushing through my eyes. "I don't feel very well, so he brought me back."

"That's good of him."

"He's a good person, Dad."

"He's a flattie, Lo. That's all I need to know."

He starts to walk and I follow him. I glance back, but Dean is gone. There's nothing to show he was even there.

Chapter Twelve

LO

After an hour of silence in the car, we set up in the new place, an empty space at the edge of town. The ground is mangled and chewed on.

"Nice," Rita says, kicking at a dirty plastic bag. Gramps says the site we pitched on last year has been pockmarked with new houses, so we've been pushed down the ladder to here.

"We won't get half an audience if they have to drive to us," Spider mumbles, as we carry heavy poles between us.

And I wonder if I care. If people don't come to see us, our circus life would stop. I could finally sow my roots and have my vegetable plot. But Dad? Rita? I think they'd shrivel up and die.

We do it all, as we always do. Inside the big top, ropes are hauled up, the floor is swept, curtains are fixed. Rita and I piece together the small wooden wall of laughing clowns and jugglers and circle it around the center ring.

"Are you going to see him again?" she asks.

"Yes. He'll come here," I tell her, but she frowns at me, so I turn away. The rolled-out air is still stale, so I step outside into the daylight, hoping there's a breeze to take my headache with it.

Ma is standing with Rob. They're talking, her face serious. He watches her all the time, the way she tucks her curls behind one ear with one hand, the way she holds a pile of costumes in the other. He tries to touch her arm, but she pulls away.

Lightning breaks behind my eyes as I head from them. I walk past the ticket booth, where Gramps is tucked safely inside, doing the one job he still can. He waves at me, and I know Dad will be even more angry if I sneak away now, but I open the door to the little wooden shack and step up.

"Come to help?" Gramps asks and there's something about his smile that makes me feel suddenly tired. I want to curl up in the warmth of his coat and go to sleep.

"To get away," I say and he nods.

"That's why I like it in here during set-up. I can hide in here for hours."

"What are you hiding from?" I ask.

"Noise. I can't hear Margaret so clearly in the rabble."

"You hear Margaret?"

"Of course. She speaks to me all the time." He takes a small bag of change from the box at his feet and sprinkles it into the till. I like the noise. It feels very real, something you can touch.

"You never told me," I say.

Gramps puts the empty bag back in the box and looks up at me.

"And I never told you that Margaret was a flattie," he says. It's as though he's unwrapping a truth and passing it carefully to me.

"My grandmother?" I say quietly.

Gramps nods. "I met her one year when we stopped for the winter. I was working on the arcades when I saw her. And I could tell straight away that I would marry her."

"I never knew."

"My parents never forgave me. Even when I didn't leave the circus, as they'd feared, even when it was Margaret who left everything and joined us instead, they wouldn't come around. They never quite accepted her."

"Dean can't join us," I tell him. "He lives alone with his mom, and he can't leave her."

"If he's the one, you'll find a way."

"Sometimes I think I want to leave," I say.

"The circus?" He raises his ragged eyebrows at me.

"Yes."

"Margaret battled with that for years. But the circus got into her blood and that was that."

"But what if I don't want this forever?"

Gramps picks up another bag of coins and tips them crinkling into the till.

"It's harder than you think to leave. There's magic here that you don't get anywhere else. There's our ways. We're different to them."

"We're not so different."

"When I was a boy, I'd think that if we stopped moving, we'd sink through the ground. That underneath the top bit of earth was quicksand."

"You told us that when we were little. Rita believed you."

"And you?"

I laugh. "I thought you were mad."

"Maybe we all are, a little bit."

I lean my head into my arms on the ledge in front of me. It's uncomfortable, next to the till, but I don't care. I feel too tired of it all, of the thinking and the rights and the wrongs, the tightrope threading my family together, which feels like it will snap under the weight of us.

"You'll be just fine, Lo," Gramps says, his hand gentle on my shoulder. I could sleep now, tucked into his words. "You'll see."

* * *

The air around the supper table is stifling. Ma eats in absolute silence and Rita chews quickly, wanting to make it over. Dad has his head bent low, weighed down heavy with the tension looping among us. I'm hungry, but the chicken is making me feel sick. I was hoping food might settle my headache, but instead the pain pushes deep into me.

When the meal is finished, I wash the plates carefully, scrubbing every scrap of food from them. Ma always tells me to wear the rubber gloves, but today I ignore her. I want my hands to wade through the soft bubbles and feel them pop to nothing against my skin.

"Spider's bringing his guitar to the barrel fire," Rita says, wiping a plate dry with her cloth. "At least out here we've got no neighbors to disturb."

"I'm not coming tonight," I say.

"You can't not come. He's been working up to this for ages."

"I'll ask him to play it for me tomorrow."

"That's not fair on him," she says.

"I'm not feeling well," I tell her.

"Rubbish. You're just wanting to show how angry you are with Dad."

I put down the sponge and don't bother to wipe my hands as I walk away from her.

"You're being selfish," Rita says. She's angry with me, but I'm too tired to fight. I want to switch off my thoughts, just for tonight.

"I'm going to bed." And I close the door on her before she can say any more.

* * *

I wake up with a sharp pain digging under my ribs. It comes on strong and then disappears, ebbing with the tide of my breath. I wonder if I've been sleeping awkwardly, pressing into my arm, but it feels different to a bruise, like something is wrong inside.

"Rita," I whisper, but she's swallowed by sleep.

The pain slips up into my head and cracks so tight in my eyes that I think I might be sick. I get up, feel in the dark for the door. Sweat sticks my T-shirt cold to my skin as I stumble into the bathroom.

I squeeze a washcloth through some water and put it wet on my forehead. Drips fall in my eyes, as I sit on the closed toilet seat. The burning in my ribs is so bad that it takes the rest of the room away. I feel for the comforting thud of my heart and try to steady the pain with its beats. But a knife is sawing through my ribs, scattering boiling splinters into my skin.

"Ma," I say, but she'll never hear me, and my words are squeezed and useless.

I get up and walk back to our room. The door rattles slightly as I open it, the light from the bathroom following me in.

"Rita?" It hurts to stand straight, to shake her awake.

"Lo?" she asks, half sitting up.

"My ribs hurt," I say.

"Your ribs?" She pushes back the duvet. She's heavy with sleep, and I wonder if I'm dreaming.

"My head hurts," I say. And the tangled sleepiness of her hair makes me want to cry.

She puts her palm to my forehead and leads me back into the bathroom. I know what she's looking for in the cupboard. I know she won't find them.

The bile in my throat rises so quick that I have to push her out of the way. I hardly lift the toilet seat before I vomit the pain from deep inside me. Rita holds back my hair, but my head hurts too much and I pull away from her and start to cry.

"Did you eat anything strange when you were with Dean?" she asks as she flushes the toilet. I shake my head. "Did he make you take something?"

"No."

"I think we should get you to a doctor," she says. She's filling the empty toothbrush mug with water and she holds it out for me. I'm so thirsty, but I don't want to be sick again. "I'm going to get Ma."

"No. Don't wake her."

"I've got painkillers under my pillow," Rita says. "I'll get them." I grab onto her hand.

"It'll help," she says.

"I had them," I say.

"Had what?"

"The acetaminophen."

"And it didn't make you better?" There's worry in her eyes.

"I took them before."

I pull my knees to my chest, but it hurts too much. I stretch my legs out, but the pain stabs so hard that I think I might be sick again.

"What do you mean 'before'?" I can see in Rita's eyes that she's already working it out.

"Last night. I took some."

She hesitates. "How many?"

"Twenty-one."

"Jesus, Lo." She crashes out of the front door. I hear her calling for Ma, for Dad. I lie on the floor and wait before Ma is here, in the doorway, in the bathroom.

"Did you take the pills?" she asks. I don't want her to know. I don't want any of them to know.

"When?" Dad is behind her, tying his shoes as he talks to me.

"Last night," Rita says. Panic drifts off her in spikes.

Dad grabs my arm and pulls me up. "What were you thinking?" he asks. "That doing this would change my mind?" Change his mind? "About you seeing Dean."

"Not now, Ray," Ma shouts at him.

"Rita, stay with Gramps," Dad says.

"I'm coming with you," she replies.

"No. You're staying here." He's half dragging me out of Terini, but it hurts so much to walk, my chest burning when my body is stretched straight.

"I want to come too," I hear Rita say, and she starts to cry.

"She'll be OK," Ma answers. "Go into our bed and try to sleep. We'll be back soon."

Dad's arms go under me and he lifts me up. The smell of him is close, and I wonder how I ever wanted to leave him.

"It's not the pills," I tell him. "That was too long ago." It's something else. I don't know what it is, but it's something very wrong.

Ma rests my head on her lap. The car smells too strong, and I want to be sick again. It moves so quickly, through the dark, street lights so bright that I have to close my eyes.

I want to see Dean. I want to see Spider.

The car stops, and they get out. Dad picks me up. We're at a hospital.

"I'll find you," Ma says. "Go quickly." And she's driving off as Dad carries me inside. I press my head into his chest, hoping he'll make the pain go away.

He stops running, and he's shifting from foot to foot.

"I need to go in front," I hear him say. And he's forcing his way past someone, my legs brushing against people.

A little girl is crying.

"We're first," a woman says firmly. But my dad pushes through and leans me against a ledge.

"She's taken an overdose," he says. And now his voice cracks and I hold him tighter as his shame seeps into me.

He's telling someone my name. That we're travelers, so we don't have an address.

"We don't have time for this," he growls.

"My head hurts," I whisper into his shirt. I breathe him in, but the pain doesn't go away.

"I'm not going to wait," he shouts.

"Dad," I say, but I don't think he hears.

They tell him to sit on a chair, but he paces with me in his arms. His muscles, his back, must be burning, but he won't let me go.

He paces and he paces and the thudding in my head is still here.

They call us into a room, and he sits down. I'm too big on his lap, but I'm a child again.

"So can you tell me a bit about what's going on?" a woman's voice asks.

"She's taken an overdose," my dad says sharply. "We need to see a proper doctor now."

"I didn't mean to," I whisper. "Not really."

"Laura." The woman touches my arm and I look up. "Was it pills that you took?" I nod. "It's very important that you try to tell me exactly what it was."

"Twenty-one acetaminophen," I say, and I feel Dad's arms tighten around me.

"When?" she asks.

"I don't know," I say. She looks up at my dad.

"Last night, I think," he says, his jaw clenched.

"A few hours ago?" the woman asks.

"The one before," I say. *There were pills in my hand and I put them in my mouth.*

"And are you sure about how many you took?" she asks. I nod.

I think I am.

But why did I take them?

"Right," she says. She puts her fingers on my wrist and we wait.

"My ribs hurt," I tell her.

"Can you show me where?" she asks and I point to my right side. She nods, takes her fingers from my wrist and types something onto her computer.

"This is to test your blood pressure," she says. She's wrapping something around the top of my arm. "Have you ever had it done before?" I shake my head. "It will start to feel a bit tight and uncomfortable, but it won't be for long." She presses a button and the blue bandage on my arm swells.

"She needs to get the pills out of her," Dad says. His chest heaves in and out. "You need to pump her stomach."

There's a beep and the squeezing on my arm starts to go.

"I'll refer you through to the doctor as soon as I can. They'll do blood tests, and the results of those will show us what we're dealing with," the nurse says. "Right, I need to take your temperature, Laura." She's holding a thermometer. It makes me want my mom, and I think I might cry again. "I'm just going to put it in your ear. It won't hurt, OK?"

"She's taken acetaminophen," my dad says, his voice a solid wall. "We need to see a doctor, now."

"I know you're concerned." The nurse tries to calm him, but I can feel his arms ticking against me. "I'll do this as quickly as I can."

I think I'm going to be sick again and I have to breathe steady through my nose. I close and open my eyes. There's a painting of a giraffe on the wall behind her. I try to count the spots on its body, but the sharp ache in my head clamps my mind tight.

She takes the thermometer from my ear.

"My head hurts," I say.

"I know. It's horrible for you. We'll give you something to help as soon as we can. Now, if you can pop onto this chair, we can check your weight."

Dad lifts me and places me on a cold, plastic seat.

"Great. We're done," the nurse says and she smiles at me before she looks at Dad. "If you could take Laura to the pediatric waiting room, it's a bit nicer for you, less crowded. It's just left outside of here and two doors down. Someone will come and get you as soon as possible."

I rest my head into him. I feel him lift me, and I keep my

eyes closed as he walks with me to a different room.

The pain is scooping me raw.

"Dad," I cry and he holds me tighter.

"Not long now," he says, and he starts to rock me. A man arrives and they put me in a wheelchair.

Ma is here, walking beside us. I let her take my hand.

In a room, Dad lifts me onto the bed, and Ma strokes my hair.

"My ribs hurt," I tell her.

"They'll give you something soon, Lo," Dad says. The door opens and it's a different woman.

"Hello, I'm Nurse Collins," she says. She's talking to none of us and all of us. "I'll be looking after you for a while." She smiles at me, but it makes my head hurt more. "You must be Laura." I try to nod. "I'm going to take a bit of blood for tests. Is that OK?" But already she's putting a tight band at the top of my arm.

Dad holds my other hand. His breathing is too quick.

"This will only hurt for a second." The nurse is speaking to me. "A little scratch." She puts the needle in my arm, and my dad holds my head so that I look away. A fish sinks his teeth in and sucks my blood.

"This is for basic liver function tests. The results won't take long, and they'll be able to show us the extent of any liver injury. And we'll be looking at something called your creatinine levels, to check how your kidneys are doing."

"Has she taken enough to do proper damage?" Dad asks, his arms going tense around me. I want him to squeeze away the pain in my head.

"The kidneys, less likely," the nurse says. "It's the liver we're more worried about. This might hurt a wee bit more,

Laura." She's holding my wrist, the tight band lower down on my arm. I try to pull away from her, but she holds me firm. "Laura, this is a really important one. We need to know if your liver is all right. And when we've done all the tests, we can give you something for the pain."

"Hold still," my mom says, and she bends down and kisses my forehead.

Another woman comes in, and I relax slightly as there's no fish by her ankles, but then one bites me on the wrist and I scream.

"I'm sorry, sweetheart," the nurse says. "This one does hurt. But we need to check your acid levels."

They're burning my blood.

"Try to keep her steady." It's the other woman talking.

"Hello, Laura. I'm Dr. Sangha," I hear her say. I look up at her, as the wave of pain begins to pass, but I can't speak. My words are caught in the net. "And are you her parents?" Ma and Dad look at her as though she's a creature they've never seen before. She focuses back on me. "I've read from your notes that you've taken some pills, Laura." I nod, as the nurse takes my arm again.

"Another small scratch," she says, and I start to cry. My head hurts and my chest hurts and no one is listening to me. I'm drowning in this strange dream. "It's all right, sweetheart. All done," and she's putting my blood away.

"Can you remember how many pills you took, Laura?" the doctor asks.

Dad's hands are clumsy as he strokes my hair, spreading smoldering coal through my skull.

How many? I pushed them into my hand, one after the other.

"Sometimes more than one," I reply.

"Do you remember how many in all?" the doctor asks gently.

"I don't know," I say.

"Twenty-one," Dad says. "She took twenty-one."

"And they were all acetaminophen?" she asks and I nod. "And it wasn't this night, but the night before?"

"I think so."

"And yesterday, did you feel anything? Did you have any symptoms?"

I shake my head. I don't think so. I don't know.

Yesterday. I want to wake up now with Dean in our starling field. Maybe he left me there and I'm waiting for him.

The nurse injects something through the tube stuck into my arm.

"This will help with the pain," the doctor says.

"She needs something to get rid of the acetaminophen," Dad says.

"I know this must be difficult for you," she answers calmly. "We have to administer something called acetylcysteine. If it's able to, it can neutralize the effects of the acetaminophen. There's always a chance that Laura is confused about how many pills she took and when she took them." The doctor looks at us. She pauses before she speaks again. "But I'm afraid that I have to warn you, the chances of the acetylcysteine working are very slight." Ma's grip tightens on my arm. "By the time it's through, we should have the blood test results, and then we can make a plan."

Dad breathes out heavily, as though he's been holding his breath all his life.

"We'll do everything we can," the doctor says. And then she leaves us. We all stare at the door, until I curl on my side, away from my mom and dad.

When I blink, my eyelashes brush the pillow. It's the sound of angels' footsteps. If they're in here, hidden in this room, they can save me.

Dean. I close my eyes and the angels walk away. Dean. I let my mom stroke my hair as I cry.

The nurse comes back in, and I turn to lie on my back.

"This is the acetylcysteine," she says, as she hangs a see-through bag filled with liquid onto a straight pole by the bed. If I was small, I could walk up it with Rita and balance on the top together. "It will work through your system quickly and we'll know soon whether it's had any effect." I watch as she straightens the thin tube running from it and clicks it onto the one sticking into my arm. "Hopefully you won't get any side effects, but there's a small possibility that it will make you feel a little sick and you might develop a bit of a rash. And if you're worried at all about your breathing, just let us know."

I fill my lungs with air. Each small breath keeps me alive. I hold my hands out, palm side up, and look at the lines that creep across my skin. They're my lines, my handprint, my fingerprints that no one else has.

Rita and I have left footprints everywhere we've been. Tucked behind rubbish bins in the town with the shrieking child, hidden in the grass in the park where the fair kept us awake all night.

"Lo?" It's Ma, looking close at me.

"Yes."

But she doesn't say anything else. She just puts my hand onto her cheek and waits for angels to come and work their magic.

★ ★ ★

The doctor looks different when she walks back in. She closes the curtain behind her and Dad holds tight to my hand.

"I'm afraid I don't have good news," she says. I watch her mouth as she speaks. The pause is filled with strange words.

"Laura, your blood results indicate severe liver damage."

"The drip didn't work?" Ma says.

"No. I'm afraid it was fighting against too much. It takes very few pills to do a lot of damage." She pauses, as though we should speak. When we don't, she sits down on the end of the bed. It makes the mattress tip, so we might capsize. "Laura, unfortunately any medicine we give you here can't help. We're suggesting transferring you to the liver unit at Kings Hospital in London." She looks at my mom. "They're in the best position to do further assessments and think about the next level of treatment."

"What sort of treatment?" Dad asks.

"It's difficult to say at this stage. They might discuss the possible option of a liver transplant," the doctor says.

"A liver transplant?" Ma falters.

"Laura?" It's the doctor's voice. She's looking at me slowly, the heavy blink of her eyes, the weight of her lashes. "Do you have any questions?"

She wants me to ask something, but I shake my head.

"Can she survive without a liver?" my dad asks, his voice an echo of his own.

"No, I'm afraid not," the doctor says.

My dad begins to slowly shatter, like a piece of china. First a few small lines appear, legs of a spider, before they spread out and his eyes, his nose, his mouth fall through the cracks.

"There must be something else you can do," I hear Ma say. Her words float like bubbles, and I pop them one by one.

"Something you can give her to make her better."

"I wish there was," the doctor says. "But acetaminophen causes acute liver failure and the damage is often irreversible."

I know I should say something, but the words get lost in the thudding in my head.

"You'll have a transplant, Lo," Dad says, his voice steel. "There'll be a liver."

I'll get someone else's liver.

"Do you have any other questions?" the doctor asks.

"How long will her liver last without a transplant?" Ma asks. The doctor pauses for a heartbeat that stretches too far around the room.

"Two or three days," she says.

I see her mouth move. I know there are words and I reach for one.

"Days?" I look at her to change it, because days are short, days are too soon.

"I'm sorry. I wish that I could say something different."

"When do we go to the liver hospital?" Dad asks.

"I'm going to arrange it now."

The doctor doesn't look me in the eye, as she flattens out the sheet on the bed and stands up.

"I think you should call anyone who would like to come and see Laura."

My dad starts breathing too quickly.

"The staff at Kings will help you arrange for them to visit."

She stops at the door. "It's a very good hospital. You'll be in the best place possible, Laura." And then she walks away again, leaving us watching the space where she once was.

"Where do they get the liver from?" I ask into the room.

My parents look at me. They seem so different—I know them and yet I don't.

"Someone gives it up for transplant," Dad says.

"But they can't live without it," I remind him.

"No," Dad says.

"So how can they give it to me?"

Dad looks as though he doesn't understand me.

"You know this, Lo," he says.

"Someone has got to die first." Ma's voice drifts toward me.

Someone dies. I live, but someone dies.

"They'll save me?"

"Yes," Dad says. "They will."

And there's silence. I notice every second ticking by. Dad stands up. "I'm going to get Rita."

He's starting to cry, but I don't want him to.

"I'll show you where the car is," Ma says quickly. She rushes out of the room before him, without looking back. Dad leans down and kisses me on my cheek. His eyes are covered in tears.

I put my arms around his neck, because I don't want to let him go. But I don't want to see him cry, and he's breaking apart on my skin.

"I've got to get Rita," he says as he pulls away from me and disappears too, leaving me alone in this room.

I stare at the ceiling. There must be layers of breaths of all the people who've lain in this bed.

I feel tears, steady on the edge of my cheek. I forget why they're here and then I remember. The doctor says my liver is failing. I put her words in a barrel and roll it across the grass toward the cliff. I push it off, watch it fly and fall and thud onto the rocks below.

The effort makes me too tired to stay awake, so I close my eyes and wait for time to come back.

"Laura, love." Someone is pressing on my arm. A woman is standing next to me, blurred by my sleep. Ma stands next to her, but it isn't my bedroom. "We're transferring you to London."

I'm in hospital.

My head was hurting and now it's not.

Layers of my mind peel back and show me that I've killed my liver. It's dying inside me. It's broken and they won't mend it.

How long?

Days.

"Ma." I grab for her hand and I pull her toward me to make the rest of the room go. I'm crying and she's trying to hold me, but my thoughts are falling over. I don't want blackness instead of the sky.

"Lo." Ma is stroking my hair and I need to hold her voice.

"I was better," I tell her. "I was OK."

"We'll find a new liver." But my mom's face is crumbling to dust.

"I don't want a new liver. I want mine to get better." I grab her hand again, because she doesn't seem to see. "We need to get a better doctor."

"You're going to a new hospital now, Laura," the woman says. "They'll do lots more tests."

"What have you done with Dad?" I ask her. He's not here. He's not anywhere in this room.

"He's fine," Ma says.

"Where is he?" I stop crying so that I can look properly at the woman.

"He's gone to get Rita," Ma says. "They're going to meet us in London."

"How will they get there?" I ask.

"Dad will drive the car."

"Can I sit with Rita?"

"They'll meet us there," Ma says. She looks so tired.

"Where's Gramps?"

"Carla is looking after him until we go back."

I try to shake the bandage from my arm, but it won't loosen.

"We'll have to be back by tonight," I tell her. "Tricks will kill us."

"We'll pop you on this," the woman says. She's standing next to a thin bed with wheels.

"Traveling in style." There's a man here too.

They make me stand up, because if I go with them I'll see Rita and my dad. I curl back down under the other sheets. The man is by my head and the woman is by my feet and they push me from the room.

Ma holds my hand as we walk down the sunken blue corridor. Its air snaps at her heels.

"You're shaking," I say. I can feel her trembling against my palm.

"I'm just cold," she says.

"You'll be warm in the ambulance." The man smiles at us, but it isn't real. I have a better pretend smile, which I use to make the hands clap.

They lift the bed into the ambulance, clicking it into place. There are wires everywhere. It makes me tired just looking at them. I can't see where one starts and another ends.

"You'll lie down for the whole journey," the woman says.

"Yes," I reply. I sit up to try to touch the little screen, and I wonder if it'll make that noise.

"If you lie down now, Laura, we'll get you comfortable."

It isn't like my soft bed. There are no wooden slats above me. If there were, I'd write a note to Rita and hide it underneath her mattress. I'd tell her about Dean but make her promise not to tell Ma and Dad.

They pull straps across my chest and legs. A man gets in.

"Hello. I'm Dr. Jones." He shakes my mom's hand. "I'll be staying with you for the journey. Is that OK, Laura?"

I nod and watch as they sit down, seat belts sucking them into the seats.

Ma isn't wearing make-up. I hear the van doors shut.

"Can we keep them open?" I ask, my heart battering too quickly now because this space is so small. Once, Spider put me in a box and taped it shut.

"We can't drive with them open," the doctor smiles.

"Where are we going?" I reach out for Ma's hand as I try to sit up. She leans over to me, her seat belt stretching.

"We're going to the hospital in London," she says.

"Where's Rita?" Panic flicks in me.

"She's meeting us there."

I'll see Rita soon. I'll wait for her there.

I don't like the wires, so I close my eyes. "Ma?" I ask. She's here, holding my hand. "Where are we?"

"We're in the ambulance."

I hear the wheels underneath us. Sleep lifts its layers from me.

"They're taking me to get a new liver?"

"Yes," she says.

I've ruined my one. It was working and now it's shutting

down and it wants to take me with it. I don't want to go. I want to live. I need to feel the weight of feathers in my hair.

"Ma." I don't want to cry. She leans close to me. I've never seen her eyes like this, fear and love spiraled so deep. She's beautiful, and I'd forgotten. I want my liver to work so I can keep seeing her. Please, please, please, don't make me leave her.

I hold her hand so tight. Feel her own bones, her own blood in its miracle stream that keeps her breathing. And I never, ever want to let her go. I want to forever see her watching over me, know that her skin will keep me safe. Know that she's mine and Rita's mom and nobody else's.

Rita. I curl my knees but the hurt doesn't go smaller. It swells so big inside me, ripping my brain, my lungs, my heart into little shreds. There's nothing left of me but hurting.

"Ma."

The doctor watches and I want to scream at him to make it stop. Make it not happen. Find the right medicine to mend me.

"Ma." The thought of her is swallowed whole by blinding darkness.

"Lo?" Ma's voice finds me and wakes me. It must be breakfast, but I'm feeling sick, and I don't think I want to eat.

I'm not at home, though.

I remember. The bitter quick taste of the pills. Dean's car. The hospital.

There's a strap across me and I can't get up.

"Ma." I panic.

"It's OK, Lo," she says as she tries to stroke my hair. I thrash against her.

"They've got it wrong," I shout at her.

The doctor stands awkward by the bed stuck into the ambulance.

"They'll hurt me," I say.

"They're trying to help us," Ma says, but she's starting to cry.

"They're wrong." A headache is seeping its way in again. It weighs my body down, washing it through with tiredness.

"This is the best place for you, Laura," the doctor says. "We're at a very good hospital."

The doors open and daylight streams through. I try to blink it away because it hurts.

They're pushing the bed with me in it. Looking at the sky makes me dizzy. We go through doors, and the moving ceiling makes me feel sick. Ma holds my hand.

"At least we don't have to battle with the lifts," the man pushing the bed says. He's above me, and it makes the world slip. "This place might look a bit old-fashioned, but you're in the best hands."

"How will Dad find us?" I ask Ma, as she walks along beside us.

"I've told him where to come."

"He'll get lost." There're too many high ceilings and thin corridors.

"He'll know how to find us."

Doors and more doors swing shut behind us.

"Here we are."

"I don't like it," I tell Ma. There's a strange smell that slithers down inside me. Ma just squeezes my hand. "My head hurts," I whisper, but I don't think she hears me.

We wait by a desk, and the doctor talks to other people, but I keep staring at the ceiling until we move without him, the smell trapped in the wheels underneath me. Through another door and into a more silent room.

"The unit is nice and quiet for you at the moment," the man from the ambulance says. There are three empty beds and a corner of the room has a curtain pulled around it.

"Where's Dad?" I ask. "Is he in there?"

"No. That's another patient. You'll be just here." The ambulance woman unstraps me. "This is your bed," she says, and they help me over onto the tightly stretched sheet. She points to the chair next to us. "Mom, you can sit here," she says and Ma nods, as though her head is moved by strings.

"We won't be here long, Ma," I tell her. "You can share my bed if it's more comfy."

She doubles over slightly, like she might be sick, but then she straightens herself quickly.

The man starts to pull the curtain around us, blocking out the room, but a woman appears just in time.

"Laura?" she asks and I nod and she looks at my mom. "Are you Laura's mom?"

"Yes." My mom's voice shouldn't be here, in this strange room.

"I'm Chrissy. I'm your intensive care nurse, so I'll be closely linked to you, and you can ask me anything." I stare at her. She looks back to me. I like her face; it's smiling, even when she isn't. "So, you're from the circus?" she asks. "I've never met anyone from the circus." Now I see her as a child, wide-eyed for us. "Do you do the trapeze?"

"Yes," I tell her. I was on the trapeze with Dean.

"I always wanted to do that. Although I'm not sure I could now, as I'm not so good with heights anymore."

We were on a roof and nothing could touch us but the clouds.

"When will you get Lo a new liver?" Ma asks suddenly.

217

"We'll do everything we can, but for now we just need to get her settled and comfortable," she says. "In a minute I'm going to hook up some machines that will keep an eye on Laura's heart and oxygen levels and tell us how her blood pressure is doing. If they decide to put Laura on the transplant list, there'll be a lot of people in to see you—an intensive care physician, your anesthetist and your consultant surgeon. But I'll be your first port of call." She looks at me. "So you mustn't worry as I'll be here. If there's anything you don't understand, then I'll help translate it for you. It can seem a bit like a foreign language."

"When will we know?" Ma asks, her face determined. "If there's a liver for her?"

"It's impossible to predict if there will be one," Chrissy says. "But she's in the best place."

Ma suddenly leaves me. She finds the gap in the curtain, and I hear her feet across the floor.

I let Chrissy take my hand.

"This is a very difficult time for you all," she says quietly. A question is at the edge of me. It tastes of salt.

"Will I die?" I look her straight in the eye, so I can see if there's the flicker of a lie.

"We'll do everything we can to make sure you don't," she says.

"But I might?" My heart beats hard at my breaths.

"It will be very difficult for us to find you a liver in time," she answers.

There must be a way. If I push really hard against the day I can turn it into yesterday and then yesterday again. I can be in Terini, I'll walk through the door and just be angry at it all, at Ma and Rob and Dean and Rita. I can find a glass and smash it hard against the wall. Watch as it shatters and leave the pieces and then run from it, just for a bit. I can run alongside the sea, the water calling to my angel wings. The wind will listen to me, and then I'll know that nothing's so bad. Nothing's so bad as this. As leaving it all, really leaving it all forever.

"Please try," I say. But the rest of my words are trapped by the pain in my throat. Chrissy puts her arms around me and it's enough to make my tears break.

My crying is everything. It rips a hole in the ceiling and shatters the sun.

I'm sleepy as they press things onto my chest and attach me to wires. They murmur by the bed, sometimes Ma's voice pushes through. But it's only when I hear Rita that I open my eyes. The room is strange, with curtains for walls and at first she looks different too, the edges of her murky. She must have been watching me and waiting for me to wake up, because when I do, she comes forward and hugs me so tight.

She's crying though, as she lies down next to me. Our faces are almost touching, and I watch her eyelashes close and open, close and open. The sunset of her eyelid, the sparkle green of her eye.

"Why did you do it?" she whispers.

"I'm sorry." No reasons seem enough now and I feel the lines of my heart break.

"Why didn't you stop?" she asks, her voice a shadow.

"I think they've got it wrong," I say. "I was fine. I took the pills, but I got better."

The sound of Rita's tears hits hard on my chest, and I hold her hand tight.

"I'm not sick enough to die," I tell her. "I'll get better." But her tears have soaked into my bones. And they fill my lungs until the snatches of air aren't enough.

I open my eyes and Gramps is sitting next to the bed. He has my hand lightly in his, the sleeve of his coat brushing my wrist.

"Lo?" he asks, as though I'm not really here. His eyes are sunken red. I blink, to try to make it all better, but none of it goes away. Gramps's mouth doesn't smile.

"I'm sorry, Gramps."

He moves slightly. "You could have talked to me."

"I know." But my words are too dry.

"Were things really that bad?"

No. Nothing is as bad as this.

"I didn't mean to do it," I say.

Outside, there is the day. It needs to slow down and split each of its minutes and split them again and again, until they reach longer than we can see.

"You're too young for this, Lo," he says.

"I'll get better," I tell him, but for the first time ever, Gramps can't look at me. In the creases on his face, I trace our memories, Rita and I standing on a shoulder each and curled up on blankets under the van, Gramps bringing us glasses of squeezed lemon. I can't leave him. I know I can't. Fear digs into me and takes my breath from me. But I must breathe. I must breathe.

"I want to change it, Gramps. I need to make it so I didn't take those pills." He shakes his head, heavy and sad. "Gramps," I say angrily because he barely moves to make it better. "You need to get Lil. Maybe in her cards it'll say. Follow what she tells you."

"Lo," he says.

"I feel sick," I say. Gramps looks quickly around him, but my stomach suddenly twists itself open. He tries to hold my head up, but the vomit falls wet from my mouth, onto my skin and the pillow and the sheet.

My mom rushes in as the smell of vomit stings the air. It plants tiny bombs inside me that make my body shake.

I want to sit up, but I have nothing left. Chrissy is here.

She moves me, and I let her.

RITA

Lo. Her name goes in a circle, taking everything else away. Lo. Lo. If I say it enough, if I think it enough, then this will all be wrong. She'll sit up, shake off the tubes they've stuck in her neck, her hand, her arms and I'll be able to see her, the real her, my sister Lo.

I sit with Ash outside of that room and stare at the wall, and I know when she walks out of there she'll laugh and say she loves me. And we'll run so far away from here that we won't feel it behind us.

But there's a deep, red pain that's grinding inside me.

I hold Ash's hand tight. We have to anchor each other as the storm will smash us against the sky if we let go.

"I don't think I can go in." The fear in Ash's eyes spills over onto me, and I feel my arms shaking.

"I'll stay with you," I tell him.

"I won't know what to say."

"Just say what you want to. Don't leave anything out." I don't know where my strength to speak comes from. "She might be asleep, but she'll still hear you."

Spider comes out of the room that hides Lo. As he closes the door behind him, his face collapses. It makes Ash's breathing go too strange. I stand up and bring him with me, but his hand pulls at mine, trying to escape.

I don't give him a choice. I half drag him through the door, across the room, and through the curtain wall, until we're here. Seeing Lo in that bed again nearly spins me away.

It's Ash who now somehow finds his strength. He steps

forward and sits on the chair. He lets go of me, so that he can hold both of Lo's hands in his.

"Lo," he says quietly. She doesn't wake up. I hadn't warned him about how her skin is a dull yellow, but if he's shocked, he doesn't show it. "I'm here." Her eyelids flicker and I know she knows. She can feel his hand and hear his voice. "You really need to come back," he says. "The performance is rubbish without you." He breathes deeply. "And we miss you."

His head drops down and he closes his eyes. I stand behind him, my hands on his shoulders.

He leans forward and kisses her on the forehead.

"I promise I'll look after Rita for you," he says, before he stands up so quickly and runs from the room.

LO

"OK, lovely?" Chrissy asks. I tip my head to watch as she presses a button on the screen and writes something on a chart.

"Am I doing well?" I ask.

"Just grand," she replies.

"I'm scared," I whisper.

I feel myself sinking into Dad's clothes as he hugs me.

"It was nice to see Dean," I tell Rita. She lies next to me on the bed, her head tucked close to the tubes in my neck.

"He wasn't here, Lo," she says.

"Will he come back soon?" I ask. My words wade through thick mud, each letter stuck to the last.

There's a pause. Maybe she hasn't heard me.

"Yes," she finally says. "He'll be back soon."

"He'll be with his ma," I say.

Rita's arm stretches along the length of mine and at the end she holds my hand.

"I wanted a garden, to grow tomatoes," I say.

Our tears ripple along the floor, they walk up the walls and fall down on us from the strange ceiling.

"You can't leave me," Rita says, her body curling into a ball next to me.

Her pain burns up my inside, turns my blood thick.

"Lo?" Rita sits straight up. "Ma! Get someone."

I should tell her that I'm all right, that I just need to breathe, but I'm fumbling for words and only letters come out.

Chrissy is here, her face calm.

"You're fine, Laura," she tells me. "Try nice, easy breaths."

The machine next to us beeps steadily. I'm not dying. I'm alive. A liver is coming and I'll go home.

Ma smooths the hair back from my face. By the curtain, Dad holds Rita. They're a pocket of fear, and I have to look away because I'm scared my breath will go again.

"Laura?" It's a man's voice that pulls me back. "Laura?" I open my eyes. My mouth is dry and I feel sick.

"I'm too hot," I say.

"I'm Dr. Jameson. I'm one of the intensive care physicians. I need to check a few things. Is that OK with you?"

Ma is sitting on the chair next to the bed. She's holding my hand, and she doesn't let go.

"I need to examine your stomach. It might be a bit uncomfortable, but it won't take long."

Already he's rolling down the sheet. He prods my stomach, but I barely feel it.

He's losing the hair on the top of his head. Bit by bit it will go.

"The swelling is basically fluid from the body going to the wrong place," he tells my ma, as though I'm not here. "Water leaks out from the arteries and veins and has settled in the stomach cavity." I'm a fish he's scooped from the sea, my bloated body stuck on a rock. "It's what we'd expect at this stage."

My mom looks at him blankly, but I know what's behind her eyes.

The curtain moves, and Rita walks in with my dad. Panic comes with them.

"She's fine," I hear Ma say quickly.

"I'm Dr. Jameson." The man turns to shake Dad's hand.

"You've been told about Laura's creatinine levels?" the

doctor asks. "And you understand that her high level is a sign of kidney damage?"

"Yes," Ma says, her voice suddenly bold.

"At this point, it's more about keeping Laura as comfortable as possible."

"Have they found a liver?" I ask.

The doctor sits down on the bed next to me. Ma has to move her arm slightly, but she keeps holding my hand tight.

"Laura, your kidneys are failing, so you would need a liver and kidney transplant. I'm afraid that the chances are very slim." His shoulders slump slightly, but he doesn't take his eyes from mine.

"If I go home, I'll get better," I tell him. I need to be in my own bed and wake up and walk down the steps of Terini. I need to climb the ladders in our big top and jump and be caught. The sticky smell of popcorn and clapping hands. If I just put on my costume, I know I'll be cured.

"You're in the only place that we can properly manage your pain," the doctor says.

I'll shell peas with Gramps and watch as dinner boils. He'll tell me his stories and I'll have time to make my own.

"I'm sorry, Laura, it's difficult to understand what you're saying," the doctor says, leaning closer to me. My mouth moves, but the words somehow lose their way.

A song starts to play in my head, one that Dad sang to us as children. *We're pirates, alive-oh.* It loops around my mind dipping in and out, taking the tune along the tracks. *Alive-oh.* It's Dad singing and Ma and Rita with her child's voice wonky and making me laugh.

The laughing sweeps me clean, along my arms and legs and charging through my belly until I'm crying.

"Lo?" Dad's voice and his arms are around me. My throat burns and breaks with tears. "I've got you," he whispers into my hair.

And he has. He's a wall and nothing can get past him. As long as he holds me like this, nothing will be able to reach in and stop my heart, because he'll be in the way.

My head suddenly jolts back. My muscles clench and turn to stone. My teeth slam shut. There's blood in my mouth and a searing pain under my skull that shakes me.

I lose my balance and fall.

RITA

Lo throws back her head sharply, and I don't know who she is. Her eyes strike open, the whites murky yellow, but she doesn't see us. She jerks against the wires and tubes, her neck twisted and stiff. Her whole body shakes, as the doctor lowers the bed flat and calmly puts my sister on her side.

"It's OK, Laura," he says, but each jolt and shock of Lo's body takes a part of me with her.

When the shaking has passed, the doctor turns Lo on her back again and pulls the sheet straight across the rise of her swollen tummy. He wipes Lo's mouth gently with a tissue, before he turns to look at us.

"A seizure like this is due to brain swelling," he says. "I'm afraid it means that we're going to have to sedate Laura. We need to prevent further seizures and think about how we can keep her most comfortable."

But if they sedate you, how will I talk to you? How will you reply?

"It means that we'll also have to put Laura on a ventilator."

"No," Ma says quietly, her eyes wide with fear.

"It's important that we do it," the doctor says gently. "To help Laura breathe. She won't be in any pain, I promise."

I look at the broken body in the bed, but it's not my sister. I try to silently tell the doctor that this is all wrong, because someone has sneaked in and hidden a stranger under the sheet.

Our Lo is sitting at home, waiting safe for us.

Tubes go into Lo's nose and sit thick and awkward in her mouth, pressing her lips wrong. There's still a bit of blood on her, from where she bit her tongue, but I'm too scared to touch the swollen skin on her face, so I don't wipe it away.

I sit on one side of the bed, with Gramps next to me. Ma sits with Dad opposite us. They are shadows. I think I'm one too.

"Dean needs to see her," I whisper loud enough for them to hear. Dad doesn't look at me. He can't take his eyes from Lo.

"He's not welcome here," he says.

"It's what Lo would want," I say. He physically recoils from my words.

"He's not coming here," Dad says.

The lines go in and out of my sister, the machines clicking and humming to keep her safe. I put my hand on the sheet to feel the up and down of her breath, the swell of air keeping her alive.

And I pray to God and to the moon and the stars to keep her with us.

You can take my eyes and my tongue and every drop of happiness I'm meant to have if you just give her life.

Dad holds Ma's hand and their heads are bowed, too heavy to look forward. Because what is there? A road without Lo?

Wake up, I tell her. *We can't do this without you.*

Her bleached white hair is flat against the pillow. She wouldn't like it to look like this, but I don't touch it.

Fight harder, Lo. You need to stay with us. Underneath her eyelids, her eyes flutter. *We're here*, I tell her.

I look at her two freckles on the top of her cheek that never go away, even in winter. Sometimes she colors them darker with a pen and sometimes she adds a third.

"Do you remember," I whisper, "when you joined your freckles with a biro and drew a balancing man on the tightrope?" She left it there for a whole performance and no one said a word.

Please get better, Lo.

Her eyes flicker and I know she hears me. But she doesn't wake up. It's dark outside, but Lo can't see it.

Open your eyes. I want you to see the stars.

I won't sleep. I need every second to watch her and hear her breathing.

Chrissy puts a hand gently on Ma's shoulder.

"I'm sorry," she says. "I don't think you have long."

Have long?

"There might still be a liver," Dad says firmly.

Silence whispers around us. In the middle, the sheet on Lo rises and falls.

"Is she hurting?" I ask.

"No." Chrissy smiles at me, but it feels out of place. We're out of place. This isn't somewhere we should be. "I promise she's not in any pain."

"But she has the ventilator. She could wake up," I say. Chrissy takes my hand and places it tight in hers.

"Laura's organs are failing, Rita. The ventilator supports her breathing and keeps her airways clear, but it can't keep her alive." *No. It's a mistake. Lo is going to open her eyes and surprise you all.*

"Keep talking to her," Chrissy says kindly, as she lets go of my hand. "She can still hear you."

Her smile goes and she walks out through the curtain and leaves us to wait for time to tick away. For the cells inside my sister to struggle and fail.

"If you get better," I whisper to Lo, "we'll grow vegetables in the van. Gramps says we can start them in small pots in the back of the car where they'll get the sun." I'm talking quickly, needing to fill every moment. "We won't be able to grow anything too big, but we could do your tomatoes. It'll be worth it, Lo. Everything will be worth it."

Ma sits next to Dad. They both have a hand on Lo's arm, above the tube that sinks into her swollen wrist. They're both holding her tight, keeping her in this world.

"And the new trick Rob has promised to show us," I whisper to her. "We can learn it, and he says we'll love it because it's dangerous."

I turn her bracelet around on her wrist, but she doesn't move. I let it fall onto the others. The sound of stars breaking.

"If you'd told me, I would've stopped you," I say. I don't want her to hear me cry, but my tears are wet against her arm.

I watch the silent lines on the screen that hold Lo to us. They look like waves, rising up together in a storm.

There's a sudden gap, and I feel the world stop.

"Lo," I say. "Keep going."

The flat line rises again. Her heart is still beating.

I hold her swollen hand in mine, trace the moons in her nails with my fingertips.

"I'm here," I whisper.

The tube breathes air into my sister, but the lines are drifting wrong.

"Chrissy?" I hear our mom ask. I glance up, at Dad holding her and the terror sitting sharp in both their eyes.

Chrissy puts her hand on my shoulder. I feel the weight of it there. Hear the click and whir of the ventilator.

On the screen, I watch as the red line falters. The waves become smaller.

"Stay with us, Lo," I hear Dad say.

But the waves disappear. And there's only a horizon, the single blood-red line of the sea.

Chrissy turns off the screen. She's turning off the ventilator, shifting silence into the room.

"No," I tell her. "You've got to leave it on for her."

"I'm sorry," she says.

"But how will she breathe? You have to help her breathe."

"Lo," Gramps says, his one word filled with fear.

"I'm so sorry," Chrissy says.

Ma is crying. She has Lo's hand clasped to her face.

Chrissy tries to put her arms around me, but I push her away.

"You can't give up on her," I beg.

"We did everything we could."

"No," I say. "She hasn't gone."

I look again at the bed, at my sleeping sister. I wait for her to breathe.

Dad leans his face next to hers and his whole body shakes with tears. But Lo doesn't move, she doesn't wake up. Beneath her eyelids, her eyes are still.

We go out of the room, so that Chrissy can take all the tubes away. I don't want to go far. I don't want Lo to be alone with a nurse she hardly knows. Instead, I stare at the blank wall, at the white paint that looks barely dry. Somewhere, my mom holds my hand. Somehow, my Gramps stands by my side. My dad sits on the floor, his knees up tight like a little boy, his head low so we can't see his eyes.

They let us go back in, on our own.

Lo lies on the bed. The sheet on her is still. I wait for it to move, but it doesn't.

Lo?

They go to her. Ma is stroking her hair back from her face, soft against the pillow. But Lo doesn't speak. She doesn't breathe.

Lo?

How can she have gone?

She is so still. I wait and watch for her to move, to speak, to smile.

Lo? I need you.

But she's silent.

Chapter Thirteen

RITA

I walk out of the hospital without my sister. They're making us leave our Lo, and we have to walk down this corridor, go through these doors, down these steps. They're expecting life to carry on when Lo's heart has stopped.

"I don't understand," I whisper to Dad. I can see his hand is holding mine, but I can't feel it. I'm somehow trapped behind a wall of glass, watching it all. "Where's she gone?" I see his fingers squeeze mine. I can't look at his face. What I saw in his eyes in that room wasn't my dad. He fell away like a castle of sand, and I can't know the hollow grains that remain.

When Lo isn't here.

I'm breathing too fast. Dad sits me down on the pavement. Where people have walked and still walk and will always walk even though Lo won't.

My stomach spasms, and I feel it now. I'm being cut from the inside out until my brain shuts it all off, and I look up at the sky at how white it is, how it watches us all.

Ma stops the car next to us. Gramps sits in the front, staring at nothing through the window. Ma gets out, a frail stick-lady.

"I can't drive," she says. Her hands, her whole arms are shaking, and I reach out to touch them, but they won't stop. A howl from an animal comes from her, and Dad tries to hold her, but she scratches out at him and pulls at her hair. She's trying to rip her soul out. I know, because I want to rip mine out too.

Ma is crying, and Dad pushes a doctor away because no one can help us.

I hold my mom and dad, and we're a triangle now, which we shouldn't be. Three sides is not enough.

My dad picks up Ma, her arms around his neck, and he puts her so gently in the car. He pulls the seat belt across her and strokes the hair back from her closed eyes.

He holds my hand and helps me up. I sit in the back, with Ma, but Lo is not with us.

The car window is hard against my forehead. I push on it. I want to push myself through, hear the glass crack, and the splinters cut into me until I bleed so much that it won't stop and I will go and join Lo.

I push so hard, but it doesn't break. It feels like a bruise spreading under my skin, seeping into my eyes. If it blinds me, I won't be able to see any of this. I won't be able to see a world without Lo and if I can't see it, it won't be happening and she'll be here, sitting next to me. I'll keep her close and never let her go again.

I reach my hand out and wait to feel her fingers in mine. I wait to hear her move and shuffle up to me and say something funny in my ear. I press my head on the glass and wait.

Dad stops the car by our site.

"I can't get out," Ma says.

"We have to," Dad tells her, but he doesn't move.

It's impossible that we're here and Lo isn't. She can't have gone. She has to be here. She'll appear, behind Terini, waving guiltily, with the smile that makes everyone forgive her.

I lie down on the seat and imagine my head in her lap. *Don't go*, I beg her. And she strokes my hair as I cry.

"Rita." Dad has opened the door and Lo disappears.

"No." If I curl myself up so small I can disappear too.

"Rita." Dad touches my shoulder, but I hold tight to the seat. I want to claw through the material, rip all of it apart. Wind myself in its shredded springs.

I feel our ma's arms around me and she starts to rock me.

"Shhh. Shhh," but she can barely breathe for her own crying.

Outside the car, there's music from the big top.

A performance is on. They've had to carry on without Lo, without us. Spider and Ash and Rob, they're all in there and they don't know. That Lo has gone and the world has stopped.

I can't see them. I shake off Ma's hand and run up Terini's steps. I open the door and close it behind me.

Lo.

I walk blind to our room.

Lo's duvet is pushed back where she left it. It was her hands that moved it like that. She was alive, she was here, she was real. She was my sister.

You will always be my sister.

I try not to move her duvet as I curl underneath it. Deep away from the ladder witch who has stolen her. The smell of Lo is around me and I hear her laugh and tell me it's a lie it's a lie it's a lie.

I'm alive, Rita. I'm alive. But where are you?

Can't you see me?

No.

Then you're not looking enough.

But I put my hands over my ears as a weight presses so heavy into my chest that I don't know how to breathe. I don't know how I'm meant to do anything or be anything ever again.

★ ★ ★

"Rita?" It's Ash's voice. I open my eyes.

Lo has gone.

The bedroom door opens, and Ash is here. My Ash. I don't move, my head on Lo's pillow, and I look at him. He crumbles into tears and kneels next to her bed and folds his arms around me.

And we hold each other, with Lo so close. There's nothing but us and this pain. Ash and me. This tiny room in this tiny van washed away from everything and everyone and all that's left are the black holes in us, filling up with tears.

Chapter Fourteen

RITA

FOUR WEEKS LATER

Dean and I leave Lo's factory behind us, and Ernest drives us and Gramps in silence to the sea. We park near our old site.

"We'll wait for you in the car," Gramps says.

Dean and I walk straight through the middle of where our tent and vans had been. There're no signs of us left, no faded grass to remind anyone we were ever here. There's nothing to show how Lo danced down the steps and ran hiding into the folds of the ring door curtains.

I stand still where our bedroom must have been, but the pain inside me is too much, and I have to run before the missing her catches me and swallows me whole.

You jumped over this wall, Lo.

I run from her memory, past the ghost of our barrel fire.

I need to keep running until my lungs have no air left and everything will stop.

Lo Lo Lo Lo Lo. Where are you?

I stop and look for her out at sea, wait for her to appear on the waves, but she doesn't come.

"Lo!" I scream, my head held back. Her name hurts my throat and I want it to. I need something to take me from the pain that's splitting my heart. "Lo!" But she's not here, and I smash headlong into a wall of tears that breaks around me, falling brick after brick on top of me, forcing me onto the sand.

Lo.

Dean puts a hand on my arm. We sit and look at the water, at the waves that keep coming and never stop, even though the world has ended.

"How?" I ask him. "How do we carry on?"

"We just do."

The sea far in the distance holds still, flat like ice. But near to us it becomes something else. I concentrate on the noise of it. Watch each tiny part come in and curl and fall and not even wait before it goes back again.

"What happens with your circus? Without Lo?"

Without Lo.

"They have to do the same set, until we close for the season in a couple of weeks."

"And then?"

"And then I don't know."

I don't tell him that I can't perform. That I haven't even walked into our big top.

"How was she at the end?" Dean asks. I look up at him as I realize what he says, and I wonder what I'll say.

"She was peaceful," I reply. He has secrets too. Am I wrong to keep this one?

"Was she in pain?"

239

"No." The sea takes my lies and curls them up, dragging them away from me.

Dean looks up at the sky.

"Did she wonder where I was?"

"She thought you came to visit her," I say quickly. He stares at me, but I hold the truth in my eyes. "She thought you were there." He presses the palm of his hands across his forehead.

"I never saw her with anyone how she was with you," I tell him. He doesn't move. "She changed when she talked about you. She was different." It's enough to make him look back at me again.

"I'd never met anyone like her," he says. I can barely hear him above the water. "She changed me too."

"Is that a good thing?"

"Yes. She changed the way I look at things. She made me see what's important."

"You didn't know before?"

"I knew some of it. But not all of it. I'm going to change my college course. I'm going to study art."

I smile at him. "Lo would love that."

There's a sound behind us and Gramps appears.

"Is there room for an old man to join you?" he asks. Dean and I move so that he can sit between us, his coat hanging heavy around him as he settles on the sand.

"Dean," he says, his voice warm, but so sad. "Did you love Lo?"

"Yes," Dean tells him.

"You chose well," he says. "And you must never regret that choice. However much it hurts now."

Pain sits so sharply on Dean's face. "I won't," he says.

He loved you, Lo. He really loved you.

"This is a part of your life, but not all of it," Gramps says.

He looks for a long time at the backs of his hands, at the rivers of tiny bones, before he looks toward Dean again. "Do you understand what I'm saying?"

"I think so," Dean says. Gramps takes Dean's hand and puts his other hand on top, as though keeping him safe.

"You have to live twice as hard for her now." He pauses and I think he's sifting through his thoughts. "And don't try to make sense of it, because you won't. Some things you just have to accept." Gramps lets go of Dean's hand and scoops up sand into his palms. It makes his skin look even older, that he's somehow part of this beach. "The pain half kills you, but in time you gather it and carry on. And you must never wish your life away, however much it hurts."

"Then why didn't Lo know that?" I ask. I've got so much anger that I don't know where it'll go.

"She did," Dean says quietly. Sadness holds him tight. "She knew it more than any of us."

He doesn't brush his tears away as he looks over the open sea, the giant stretch of it going further than we can imagine. Maybe Lo is there, somewhere. I was looking at the top of the waves, but maybe she's hidden in them.

Are you, Lo?

I stare at the impossible stretch of it, where it meets the sky. My eyes hurt for searching.

Gramps lets the sand fall from his hand, before he puts one arm over Dean's shoulder and wraps the other around me.

"You can't see it now, but you will both be all right. You'll never stop missing her, but you'll find your way through."

"I don't want to do any of it without Lo," I say.

"You will," Gramps says. And we sit together waiting, watching the sea curling its white onto the beach.

Chapter Fifteen

RITA

"Lo wanted me to give you this," Spider says. We're sitting with Ash in his room. My place of safety these days.

"What is it?" I look at the envelope in his hand, but I don't want to touch it.

"I don't know." The shock he's waded through over the last few weeks is beginning to lift, but his eyes are still creased with sadness. "I promised I'd wait a while before I gave it to you."

He holds out the envelope, and I see that the back of it is stuck down, a wobbly kiss is drawn where the join is.

"Lo did it?"

"Yes."

I look at the biro cross and then up at Spider. We just stare at each other, trying to work out how it all happened, how it came to this. The missing her is still so big, pushing us back against the walls and squeezing out the air.

Spider passes me the envelope, but it shakes so much in my hands.

"Do you want to be on your own?" Ash asks.

"No. I need you both here," I say. He puts his hand on my arm and it calms me. I wish Lo could see Ash now. How strong he is. How he stops the earth from cracking in two.

I don't tear Lo's kiss in half. Instead I rip a small hole in the corner of the envelope and carefully open the top. I breathe courage deeply into me before I pull out the letter. Little squares of folded paper fall from it. Each has a number written on. I smile, without realizing it.

Spider watches me silently as I open the letter.

"It's not her handwriting." I feel cheated.

"She dictated it to the nurse," he says. "But it's all her words." It's only three sentences.

These are for you. Open one a week. Promise me you'll do them.

I pass the note to them. I think I'll see confusion when they've read it, but instead Spider smiles.

"That's our Lo," he says, his voice so sad that I feel my skin split and his pain sinks into mine. Every cell inside me feels made of jagged stones. I never thought it'd be possible to survive hurt like this.

"Here's the first one," Ash says. He passes me a folded piece of paper with "1" written on the front. I look at it floating strange in my palm, but I don't want to open it. I'm scared to find Lo tucked into the white, but even more frightened that she won't be there.

"Do you want me to do it?" Ash asks gently and I nod. He takes it from me, and I watch his fingers open it.

"Find me in a river," he reads. I look at him, waiting to understand the words.

"Well it was never going to be something normal, was it?" Spider shakes his head, smiling again.

"But how will she be in a river?" I ask.

"We'll just have to find out," Ash says. He seems so certain, that somehow it makes sense, when nothing else does. "We could go tomorrow. I'll ask my mom if she can drive us."

Tomorrow? It seems too far away. Lo took normal time with her and we're left with days and minutes that stretch endless and aching.

"OK," I say, though my thoughts are washed through.

Spider carefully picks up Lo's note and her little squares of paper and tucks them safely into the envelope.

"One a week," he says. "No cheating." And he hands me my sister's words. He cries so quietly and so often these days that I don't think he even notices as he stands up and turns his back toward us, walks out of the door without Lo by his side.

Ash and I stare into the emptiness. Shapes are here somewhere—the outline of his coat hanging on its hook. The light switch that his mom still cleans for him. His curtain hanging soft against the hard glass.

"They're all waiting by the barrel fire," Ash reminds me quietly. He puts his hand in mine, anchoring me so that I don't float away.

"I'm not ready."

Ash wipes my tears. "You can do this."

"I can't, not without Lo." The barrel fire will be stripped bare with her not there.

"You can."

My heart is sewn tight with sadness.

"I want to see her," I say.

"I know." He lowers his head.

"I'm so tired, Ash." Since Lo has gone, I've spent my nights curled up on Mada's sofa, counting the seconds until sleep eventually comes and waking before even the birds.

Ash looks up at me as he gets up. He doesn't give me a choice as he helps me stand. He leads me to the door, but I hesitate as he opens it. The world beyond it is too big, too empty, and I feel so lost.

"I'm scared," I say. From here I can see the barrel fire tucked amongst the dark. I know they all sit there, even Lil. Everyone but Ma and Dad who are locked so tight in their grief that they find it hard to even speak.

"I'll be with you," Ash says.

I can feel Lo's words against my palm. *These are for you.* And I let Ash lead me down the steps.

Everyone stops speaking as we approach. Spider moves up for us, and we sit on the log. Tears are on his cheeks. The grass seems to tilt, but Ash puts his arm around my shoulder to stop me from falling.

We all just stare into the flames.

"I miss her," Sarah says. She's tucked safe into her dad, Baby Stan sleeping in Carla's arms.

"I do too," I tell her.

Gramps is never normally by the barrel fire, but tonight he sits close to Tricks, his eyes unmoving from the dark sky above us. And Rob is here, but I feel nothing when I look at him. No love, no hate. There's no space for anything in me apart from Lo.

"How's your mom?" Helen asks. She's huddled close to Ernest, their hands locked together.

"She's not good," I say. And they're all silent again. Because what do you say when we're all here, but Lo has gone?

Spider picks up a stone and throws it into the fire. It knocks the flame crooked, before hitting inside the edge of the barrel. And the fire rearranges and carries on, the stone hidden out of sight.

I feel the familiar sharp pain of tears in my throat, but I squeeze Ash's hand to stop them.

Tricks coughs slightly.

"We were discussing the performance," he says. "About how we carry on next season without Lo."

"I don't want to," Sarah says, cutting his words short. Stan just hugs her closer.

How will I put on my circus skin when I'm still too scared to touch it?

"It would feel wrong," Spider says quietly. He doesn't sound like himself any more. The spark in his voice has gone.

"Rob?" Tricks asks. But Rob just looks up at him as though he can no longer see.

"I don't know how we can," Helen says.

The circle of the barrel fire breathes in all the words, takes the lifeblood of our circus and burns it to dust.

"Maybe." It's Gramps's voice that flickers in the darkness.

"Maybe we have a duty to carry on." I look at him and see only the empty space where Lo should be. "Because we are the ones who are still here."

He stops talking, the tears reaching from him, ready to meet my own.

"I think we do," Tricks says, his voice wavering.

There's a silence and I wonder if they realize they're all watching me. All except Gramps, who now looks for Lo in the stars above.

"Yes," I say, feeling Ash's hand tight in mine. "Yes," I answer for all of them. "It's what Lo would want."

And I know it is. Because through it all, she had our circus woven into her soul.

"We should do a performance with Lo at the center of us all," Carla says.

I see people nodding, the mumbling of agreement.

"We'll have to fill it with laughter then," Stan says. "And mischief."

"And storms," Carla says. She watched Lo grow from a baby. Saw her bathe in puddles and catch raindrops on her fingers.

"You could never drag her in from the lightning."

"And stars," Tricks says. "Remember when she filled the ring with cut-out stars, so she could see what it was like to walk in the sky."

"Mist. And feathers. And boys," Lil says. Her skirt sits huddled around her, growing up from the ground. She hasn't looked at her cards since Lo has gone.

"Truth and honesty," Spider says suddenly, strong in the fire-breathed air. "Lo told me to trust people. And to be brave." His mom looks at him and nods slowly.

There's a silence, and I know they wait for me.

I stare into the barrel at the center of us all, watching the flames spike and dance. Everyone still looks at me, waiting for me to tell them about my sister. But how do you share the sun and the waves and the horizon?

"She was our Lo," is what I say. But it's not enough. I curl my fingers tight around her letter in my hand. *Open one a week. Promise me.* "We'll carry on living, for her."

★ ★ ★

247

Lo would have loved this day. The bright shine in the air, the damp cold caught on the wind. I watch it all, as Carla drives us to the river.

"There." Spider points to where a thin wall of water slides down to disappear below.

"I'll find somewhere to park," Carla says. I don't take my eyes from the waterfall, turning in my seat as it vanishes behind the trees.

Carla moves the car half onto a bank and turns off the engine. Spider, Ash, and I get out onto the soft, mossy ground, the sound of leaves touching the air.

"What if she's not here?" I ask.

"She will be," Ash says, and he holds my hand safe in his. "We won't be long," he tells his mom and she nods but won't look at us, and I know she's trying to stop her tears.

The trees are thick with shadows as we push through them. It's another world in here, the smell of damp earth, the colors darkened. I touch every tree I pass, needing to feel the rough bark on my skin. I want to walk slowly, quietly, so we won't miss Lo if she appears.

The burst of light is instant the other side. And there's the river waiting for us, catching a small waterfall. We stand and watch it, Ash, Spider, and I, how it stops when it reaches a rock, but then finds a way around and swims on quickly.

"Can I drink it?" I ask. The water looks so clear, with stones patient at the bottom.

"I don't see why not," Spider says.

I let go of Ash's hand and kneel down close to it. It moves past my fingers, dampening them with cold. I make a cup from my hands and catch some of it. I had expected it to taste clean, but it's metallic and rusty in my mouth.

"It's disgusting," I say. It's the first time I've heard Spider laugh since Lo left us.

"I wonder what Lo sprinkled in it," he says. And it's there, the reason why we came.

"She's not here," I say.

"She is," Spider insists. "We're just not looking properly." He takes off his shoes and steps from the bank into the stream, the water soaking through his jeans. "I'm going to the waterfall."

"It's not exactly a waterfall," Ash says.

"It is," Spider says. "Lo would think it's perfect."

The water drags heavy and cold against my jeans, the stones underneath me made of ice.

"Come on," I call to Ash. I need him close, so he follows us too. We wade through, the stream touching up to our knees, Ash shouting the cold like a madman into the air around us.

The sound changes as we get closer to where the line of water streaks headlong down the rock. Spider is first and he stands in the mess of bubbles close to where the water falls, presses his hand through to touch the rock behind. He makes it spray in all directions, ducks down his head, laughing as it hits into his eyes.

I go quicker to meet him, put my hand next to his, feel the rush of water hit my skin. I'd forgotten what it feels like to laugh and I let the sound and the feeling hit into the water too, as it covers my clothes, my hair, my skin with cold stars.

"She's here, isn't she?" I ask Spider.

"Yes." His smile is wide.

I know that she is. I can feel her next to me, I can feel her watching in the trees, she's sitting on the rocks and diving in the river. And I know she'll always be with me.

"I found you," I whisper.

"I'll keep my promise," Spider suddenly says. "I will, Lo." He looks up to the sky through the sound of the waterfall.

I don't ask him about his secrets, but I take Lo's hand and hold it so tight.

I see myself push my arms into sequined sleeves, pulling the loop at each end over my fingers. I know I'll find Lo balanced on the silver wire. We'll be together, caught high on the trapeze. I'll see Lo as I fly through the air.

And she will be there, ready to catch me.

★ ★ ★

The cold only hits me as we scramble back up the bank. Spider is already heading back through the trees.

"Wait," I tell Ash.

"Are you OK?" he asks.

"Yes."

I am. Aren't I?

I hold his hand and take him back to the very edge of the river.

"What is it?" he asks.

The sky up above us is star-bright white. The ground underneath us holds us steady.

You can do this, Lo tells me.

"I want us to leave our footprints," I say.

Ash looks at me, his eyes filled with a million words.

"OK," I hear him say.

So I lift one foot, feeling the other press strong next to Ash's on the ground. When I topple slightly, Lo holds me safe.

I promise we'll burn bright for you, I tell my sister.

And together, Ash and I leave our footprints.

Acknowledgments

There are so many people who are the pieces of the jigsaw that made this book whole:

Firstly, my mom, who fought so hard to stay with us and gave us precious extra years. I love you, and I know that you're still with me every step of the way.

Thank you, Miles, for listening to my self-doubt and somehow always finding the right words. And to Frank, Arthur, and Albert—thank you for making every day brilliant.

To Philip, Lara, Emma, and Anna—you are sibling gold! And to my nephews and nieces—Annie, Tobia, Freddie, Harry, Tilly, Amelia, Joshy, Oliver, George, Sammy, and Johnny—for putting up with the tea-towels and dancing.

To my friend and fabulous agent, Veronique Baxter, where all my books start—this one wouldn't have ended without you. Thank you for keeping me going—your belief and encouragement means the world to me. And to all the wonderful team at David Higham—especially the lovely Laura West—thank you!

To my truly amazing editor, Ali Dougal—thank you for wanting Lo's story to be told. And for not just holding my hand but dragging me to the finishing line! I learn so much from you, and you make me a better writer every day. Thank you also to

Rachel Mann—you were so in tune with me straight away and your editorial input was invaluable. And Amy St Johnston—thank you for being so patient with all my last-minute changes and wobbles!

To the rest of the brilliant team at Egmont—I'm so proud to be with your publishing house. Especially to my star-shine publicist, Emily Thomas—my Rescue Remedy in human form! Thank you, Cally Poplak, for welcoming me with so much warmth and support. To Laura Bird and Janene Spencer—thank you for creating my beautiful cover. And thank you, lovely Tiff Leeson, for all your support.

Thank you also to my copy-editors whose detailed brains never cease to amaze me—especially Susila Baybars—you went above and beyond when technical issues melted me.

Thank you to my editor-in-waiting Ffion Edwards—you will be a brilliant addition to the publishing world! And thank you also to Nancy Hornby and Ellis Rossiter who read early chunks when I was panicking—your feedback was perfect and all of it was integrated into the final book.

To Tony Sharp—thank you for taking the time to talk with me about the wonderful circus life you shared with your wife, Maria. Thank you, Mari, for answering my endless stream of medical questions—even when balancing Gwilym on your hip in the middle of a camping field! And to Dr. Chris Nicholson—thank you for your feedback and advice. I hope that Lo's story will stop at least one person ending up as your patient.

To Miss Madras and Mr. Trotman—the books you taught me are among my favorites to this day—thank you for being inspiring teachers and soldering my love of words.

Thank you Lucy for your friendship—and for long meals

with your beautiful family—Martyn, Oliver, Finn, and Ava. And to my Rooty Toots, for love and laughter.

Thank you, Nikki, for turning me into a mermaid and to the rest of my brilliant writing group—Suzanna, Sandi, Lucy, Debs and Allie. And the people who make my world tick happy—the wonderful Whinneys, our Cameroooons, Stephen M. Nash, Abi, Er, Wally, Helen, Sarah, Laura Treneer, Shanaz, Nick M-M, Andrew, Jo Sykes, Becky, Sam, Rosie, Francoise, Fabia, Cathy, Carlene, Ula, Ian, Karen, Karolina, Helen Benson, and Lou.

To Oliver and Lucy Lapinski—your support means so much. And a big thank you to all of the amazing bloggers— especially my friend Michelle Toy (Tales of Yesterday), Grace Latter (Almost Amazing Grace—but it should just be "Amazing Grace"), Lisa (City of YA Books), Viv Dacosta (Serendipity Reviews), and to all those at Maximom Pop Books. And to Jules, Ness, and Naomi who run the fabulous Book Nook— where I could happily live.

To Jason Brown, "one of the good guys," who left this earth too young.

And finally, to my writing spirit—you held on tight as I put you through the wringer. It wasn't an easy path, but thank you for staying by my side and leading me along it.